Hearts
UNBROKEN

Hearts UNBROKEN

CYNTHIA LEITICH SMITH

CANDLEWICK PRESS

Hesci. Herein, a few words and sentences are written in Mvskoke, the language of the Muscogee (Creek) Nation of Okmulgee, Oklahoma. A glossary is included on page 295.

Neither the Indigenous nor foreign languages are italicized or translated in the main body of the text, except to indicate emphasis.

First paperback edition 2020

Library of Congress Catalog Card Number 2018959673
ISBN 978-0-7636-8114-2 (hardcover)
ISBN 978-1-5362-1313-3 (paperback)

20 21 22 23 24 25 TRC 10 9 8 7 6 5 4 3 2 1

Printed in Eagan, MN, U.S.A.

This book was typeset in Berkeley Oldstyle.

Candlewick Press
99 Dover Street
Somerville, Massachusetts 02144

visit us at www.candlewick.com

For Christopher

Falling Hard

Half past nine a.m. in the residual haze of my junior prom, I ducked into a powder room off the kitchen at the swanky lake house where the after-party took place.

It reeked of vanilla oil and was decorated with dead starfish.

Then I tapped my phone to update my newish best friend, Shelby Keller. We had texted off and on the night before, but this morning's conversation mandated face-to-face communication. She answered with "Good morning, Louise. Please tell me you didn't waste your maiden voyage into sexy fun time on that narcissistic player you call a boyfriend."

"Not even," I whispered to Shelby. "You know how Cam has to eat an entire cow or something every three hours? After the dance, we detoured to IHOP for a snack. On the way out, he threw up a whole bottle of champagne and a double-blueberry short stack in the parking lot. Then he passed out in the limo."

Her snort-laugh burst through the tiny speaker.

I replied, "Yeah, well, I may never eat pancakes again." After all, unbuttoning your semiconscious boy-friend's vomit-splattered shirt isn't any girl's prom-night fantasy.

"Sounds like I didn't miss much," Shelby said. With her part-time waitressing gig, she didn't have much time to socialize. And her earnings went to necessities, not party dresses.

"Definitely not," I said out of loyalty, though the actual dance had exceeded all expectations. "Cam and I are supposed to be at brunch in a half hour, and he's still out cold."

"Drooling?" Shelby asked.

"Snoring," I admitted.

Her laugh was less affectionate than mine.

The lake house decor was high-dollar rustic. The quarter-back, Blake Klein, is one of Cam's closest pals, and it's Blake's family's second house. Not a trailer or hunting cabin—we're talking steam room, a Sub-Zero refrigerator, and a motorboat in the detached garage. (It's not so much on the lake as near the lake.)

I didn't doubt that they had a maid service, too, but Mama raised me to be a considerate guest. Besides, having ventured into the family room, I was mindful of how whatever was left lying around might affect (for better) the boys' reps and (for worse) the girls'.

While I was talking to Shelby, the other post-prom stragglers had already vacated the premises, including the unidentified human-shaped lump under a chenille throw on the sofa.

So I tossed the scattered beer cans and red plastic cups. I retrieved and repositioned the couch pillows, wiped down the immense black granite counters, and used salad tongs to remove the condom wrappers littering the rugs. Then, after clearing more plastic cups and a few stray Doritos from the deck, I finished the job by hauling out the trash.

Finally I returned upstairs to Cam. The night before, I'd crashed on the faux-distressed leather chaise longue in front of the bay window. He was still sprawled diagonally and bare chested on the king-size bed. Not his finest moment, but it didn't matter. I was smitten.

On our first date, back in January, I'd mentioned that I'd only just recently moved to northeast Kansas from central Texas. I'd been convinced that Cam was all but ignoring me in favor of the basketball game on the sports bar TVs. Then, come Valentine's Day, he'd given me a sterling silver souvenir charm in the shape of a longhorn.

He'd been *listening* to me, *even though there had been a game on.*

"Wake up." I jostled his foot. "We're going to be late."

Cam's parents, the Ryans, were cohosts of the annual post-prom brunch (by which I mean annual for East Hannesburg High School students whose families belong to the country club, along with their preferred teammates and their respective dates).

"Check your messages," I said. "I bet your mother has already texted you."

Cam squinted at the rotating ceiling fan and reached out his hands. "Lou, save me."

"Are you hungover or still drunk?" I asked.

"Drunk with your beauty, drunk with your booty."

"You can't reach my booty from there." I clapped loudly four times. "Up and at 'em, cowboy. Take heart: there will be food."

"I can't get up," Cam whined. "Help me, Loulou."

I hated when he called me that. But the night before, we'd dined on bacon-wrapped filet mignon at Pennington's Steakhouse and swayed to classic Rihanna on the dance floor. By the magical light of the mirror ball, Cam had declared his love.

It was heady, intoxicating, being in love. So far as I was concerned, we could've stayed at the lake house all day, except for his parents.

"Shower! Now!" I risked taking his hands, and Cam, laughing, yanked me down on top of him. He tickled my sides. I curled up, trying to protect myself, but I was laughing, too.

Cam's mother greeted us in the posh country-club lobby. "Louise, dear! Don't you look pretty this morning? How was the dance?"

Before I could reply, she added, "You'll have to excuse Cam so we can have a brief word. Family business, you understand." She gestured with her Bloody Mary toward the reserved private dining room. "Don't miss the crepes station."

Crepes! I crossed the mosaic tile floor to the freestanding sign: EHHS PROM BRUNCH.

From the arched double doorway, I wandered in, marveling over the colorful art-glass chandelier, the crisp white table linens, the carved ice bowl of peel-and-eat shrimp, and the party of fifty or so, chatting, toasting, and taking photos. In addition to the crepes, I weighed the merits of an omelet station, a prime rib station, a silver platter of lox shaped like blooming roses, and a mirrored, five-tiered pyramid display of succulent-looking fruit.

I'd never been to a wedding with such a fancy, expensive spread—let alone a Sunday brunch. Don't get me wrong. My family isn't poor. I guess you'd say we're *middle* middle class.

We'd moved to East Hannesburg, Kansas, immediately after the previous Christmas, between my junior-year semesters. It didn't feel like home yet, not the way Cedar Park, Texas, had.

Definitely not the way Indian Country, Oklahoma, does.

I'd plucked three chilled shrimp from the sculpted ice bowl and served myself some smoked salmon and sliced cantaloupe when Cam's hand cradled the small of my back.

He steered me toward the prime rib station. "I'm starving," he said.

"What was all that about?" I asked, deciding to save crepes for dessert.

Cam leaned in. "My brother got engaged. Mom wants me to talk him out of it."

"What's wrong?" I asked. "She doesn't like Andrew's fiancée?"

"My mom barely knows her," Cam said. "But the girl's not exactly my mother's idea of future daughter-in-law material."

He lowered his voice. "Get this. She's only twenty, and she already has a one-year-old kid. Can you imagine the bride's baby daddy showing up at a Ryan family wedding?"

This from the seventeen-year-old guy who I'd planned to have sex with the night before. The one who'd left it to me to bring the condoms — not that we'd ended up needing them.

"Your mom will get over it," I said. "As long as Andrew's happy—"

"I don't think so. The girl is a Kickapoo Indian, so you know. She works at a coffee shop on Massachusetts Street in Lawrence."

We got in line for the carving station. "So . . . I know she's a barista?"

"Let's be real," Cam replied. "She probably took one look at Andrew and saw dollar signs. Why else would she be working at a place like that, if not to hit on college guys?"

I maintained a conversational tone. "Why would she be working at a coffee shop? Off the top of my head, I'd say it's convenient to where she lives or she enjoys interacting with the public or she believes in the power of caffeine. Maybe she's putting *herself* through college."

"Mom says *Kickapoo* sounds like a dog. Like *cockapoo* or *peekapoo*. Get it?"

I got it. The three senior couples ahead of us in line for beef were chatting sororities, fraternities, rush, and legacies. Cam joined in their Greek alphabet soup of conversation.

Meanwhile, *my* Native identity appeared to be nowhere on his radar.

Cam mentioned that his grandfather, father, and older brother were Sigma Nus at the University of Kansas. "It'll piss off Dad if I end up pledging another frat," he said with a calculated glance at his parents' table. "But I'm going to keep an open mind."

It was a discussion we'd had before, mostly, I suspected, so that when Cam finally accepted the bid from Sigma Nu, he could at least pretend he was his own man.

Once the other couples had moved on, I reminded him, "I'm Native." I pointed at myself. "One Muscogee (Creek) Nation citizen, live and in person, right here."

Cam offered me a gold-trimmed white plate from the tall stack, and I shook my head.

"You know how my mom is," he said. "She's obsessing over what people will—"

"What if it was me?" At his perplexed look, I clarified, "What if she was freaking out because you got engaged to me?"

"Are you proposing, Loulou?" Cam chuckled. "Shouldn't you be down on one knee?"

It was like he was determined not to take me seriously.

"Uh, sir?" A slender guy in his early twenties stood poised at the carving station. Jake, according to his name tag. "Sir, if you want your beef served on that plate, you'll need to give it to me. What I do is take one of these plates here"—he gestured to the stack—"place a cut of meat on it, and then present it to the guest."

Which made more sense and was clear from the station configuration. We simply hadn't been paying attention.

Cam never loved being told he was wrong, and now two people were correcting him at the same time. "God!" Ignoring Jake, he held on to his plate. "Girls are so sensitive."

My WASPy boyfriend drew himself up, emphasizing the height and girth difference between us. "Look, Louise, I'm sorry if you have a problem with . . . whatever. But I'm a good guy. And, like I've told you, I'm part Cherokee on my mom's side. Don't get all—"

"Sanctimonious?" Fact: he's not a citizen of any of the Cherokee nations. He can't name a single Cherokee ancestor who was. I profoundly doubt he's even a distant descendant.

Cam's entire basis for conveniently claiming Cherokee heritage is a combo of uninvestigated family mythology and the fact that his occasionally insufferable mother is proud of her bone structure. He'd never identify as Indian when it could cost him something.

"Whatever," Cam said again. "Do you really want to fight at prom?"

No, and in fairness, Cam had been mostly parroting his mom's talking points.

"Excuse me, sir. Beef?" Jake asked again.

Two junior couples had come up behind us since he'd spoken last.

At the interruption, Cam did a double take but handed over the plate. "Unclench," he said to me. "It's not like you're *Indian* Indian. You live in East Hannesburg. Your dad is a dentist."

"What does any of that have to do with it?" Not me talking. The guy with the knife.

"None of your fucking business," my boyfriend said, reaching to seize the plate of newly sliced, bloody meat.

Ninety-eight percent of the time, Cam radiates charm. He's the all-American golden boy, six foot five, with a promising football future. But that other two percent . . .

"Cam?" I turned away, defusing the situation. "Let's say hi to your dad. He's probably wondering why we haven't gone over there yet."

I appreciated Jake's solidarity. It was all I could do not to flash him an apologetic smile. But Cam seldom backed down, the slightest gesture could trigger his jealousy, and I didn't want anyone getting fired on my account.

Across the room, the Ryans reigned over a half dozen other parents at a large round table. The women were talking landscape architects. The men were talking golf.

It never failed to amaze me how fast my boyfriend could slip on his public face.

Cam gave me his plate to hold so he could shake hands with the dads, flirt with the moms, and bask in glowing forecasts about his senior-year game.

We'd bickered before. Usually about the way he puffed himself up or talked about other girls or cut off whatever I was trying to say. The burden fell on me to soothe him, to keep the peace. I knew Cam considered the matter closed, and he'd act incredibly put out if I raised it again. But I was tired of his ego and his attitude.

I still loved Cam, but I didn't like him very much. I'd defer only for the moment, for the sake of the occasion and the hefty parental presence.

Mrs. Ryan glanced over at my plate. "Is that all you're having, Louise?"

I could hear the admiration her voice. (The woman lived almost exclusively on vodka, raw veggies, and low-cal protein bars.) I wondered if Andrew's Kickapoo fiancée would ever find herself on the receiving end of such an approving tone.

I spoke up. "Yes, ma'am. I've had enough."

Spirit Rising

"Damn it, Lou!" Two hours later, Cam pounded the steering wheel of his SUV, which was parked in my driveway. "Stop being so dramatic. I can't second-guess every fucking word that flies out of my fucking mouth. If you pick, pick, *pick* at every goddamn little thing and ignore what I'm really trying to say, *you're* the one who's not respecting *me* enough to listen."

I opened the passenger-side door. "I'm not going to let you turn this around on me."

"I can't believe you," he shot back. "And after all the money I spent on prom!"

I jumped out and ran into my house, into Mama's waiting arms.

That evening, I could tell from Cam's barrage of texts and voice mails that he had written off what had happened as just another spat. He made some half-hearted apologetic noises, blaming PMS for my moodiness. He piled on the flattery, claimed our relationship had been "moving in the right direction," and declared that he wanted to get "back on track," which was his way of saying he still wanted sex. But after talking to Mama and Shelby, my decision was confirmed.

The New Girl who Cam Ryan had put on the social map was going to dump him.

I was dreading it. I didn't want to hear him explain how manipulative I was or how dramatic I was or how I wasn't that hot anyway or how he'd been so patient with me and I was so ungrateful and a nobody without him. I didn't want to hear him whine about all the girls he could've been with when we were together, how he'd sacrificed by staying loyal.

Should I send a text? No, too casual. He might think I was kidding.

A letter? No, his mom might screen his snail mail.

She *would* screen his snail mail.

E-mail, I decided. Never mind that the only people I e-mail regularly are my grandparents and a couple of my great-aunties. Football may be Cam's signature sport, but he's also on the baseball team, just for kicks. The head coach routinely e-mails the team, so Cam checks his account daily.

I hauled myself out my bed and logged on to my laptop.

I thanked Cam for the good times. I wished him the best of luck this season.

As gently as possible, I said we were over for good.

At a quarter till ten, I pushed Send.

Monday morning, before the bell, I returned to the sign-up sheet for Cheer tryouts on the door of the girls' locker room. I grew up with the cheerleaders in central Texas, and I missed being one of them. I'd been looking forward to joining the East Hannesburg squad.

(That might sound presumptuous, but EHHS Cheer is nowhere as competitive as Cedar Park Cheer.)

The appeal? Gymnastics, dance — I've taken jazz and ballet since I could walk. I enjoy the sense of belonging that comes with participating in a team sport. Plus a cheerleading uniform doubles as social armor and eliminates the pressure of figuring out, day-to-day, what to wear. All you have to do in exchange is kick, punch, chant, blend.

On the other hand, making the squad would also ensure that Cam and I went to the same parties, had the same friends. The kind of friends I'd always had.

My move to Kansas had been a new beginning. Life without Cam was another one.

I scratched my name off the tryouts list.

To hear Cam tell it, *he'd* ended our relationship because I'd butted into his personal family business. His friends agreed that I'd been out of line. Clingy. Controlling.

I didn't blame them. It's always easier, letting Cam have the final word.

But not everyone was a fan.

Shelby and I had clicked because she's no-nonsense. She takes the world as it comes, not as if it belongs to her. She's different from Cam's crowd that way.

After school, Shelby posted a printout of his profile pic on the dartboard at the local pub where she waitresses. "Embrace the catharsis." She handed me a fistful of ammunition. "You're a woman scorned."

"I don't feel scorned," I assured her, aiming a dart at the target. "And I have lousy hand-eye coordination. I could kill someone."

Gesturing large, one of the Grub Pub regulars accidentally whacked over his beer pitcher, soaking the loudly feuding middle-aged couple at the next table.

"Don't sweat it." Shelby jogged to do damage control. "We could stand to lose a few!"

Estvmin Like Cet Towa?

In June, my family road-tripped to Oklahoma for the annual Mvskoke Fest in Okmulgee. We're talking parade, stomp dance, softball, rodeo, walk/run, games and sports tournaments (traditional and not), scholarship pageant, music, food, and pony rides for the little kids.

I'm an urban—make that *sub*urban—Indian. Unlike my parents, I've never lived full-time in my own tribal community. But it's home.

"I should get in shape for bronco riding," Daddy joked, then took another bite of Indian taco.

Mama tucked in a smile and patted his tummy. Quite the diplomat, my mother.

In fairness, Daddy still carries a lot of muscle on his broad frame. After more than two decades in the army, he was just beginning to enjoy the more relaxed pace of civilian life.

My brother, Hughie, was less than a month out of middle school. He used a paper napkin to wipe sweat from his brow. "Lekothe tos."

"Warm?" I blew out a long breath. "More like sweltering. Try: Oren hiye tos."

After my parents finished eating, they left to pick up Great-Aunt Sis from the doctor. Once they were out of hearing range, Hughie asked, "Do you ever wish we'd moved here?"

"Sometimes," I said, savoring my honey-sweetened fry bread. "But we have cousins back in Kansas, too, and we visit Oklahoma as often as we can." We already had plans to come back in mid-July. "Do you miss Texas?"

"I miss the Tex-Mex, especially the migas. And my friends. The bullies, not so much."

"You were bullied?" I'd had no idea, and I could've sworn Hughie told me everything.

He began tying his clear plastic straw in a knot. "A couple of years ago, the guy sitting behind me in Texas History was making 'war whoops' whenever the teacher mentioned the Comanche, so I told him to shut up.

"After that, he and his friends started whooping whenever they saw me. They thought it was funny. Then they thought it was funny to start roughing me up on the walk home from school."

He was my kid brother. My responsibility. "I could've come to get you," I said. "I—"

"It's over now," Hughie reminded me. "I'll never see those jerks again."

• • •

We stayed an extra week and visited Checotah, Eufaula, and Tulsa. Mama and Daddy also took us to pay our respects at the Oklahoma City National Memorial and Museum.

We spent quality time with our grandparents, our great-grandfather, and our great-aunties and uncles. Which is another way of saying that we spent a lot of time listening.

Along the way, Hughie and I logged a few hours with the Mvskoke language app. My brother had already decided that next summer he'd apply to Mvskoke Language Camp.

Cokv kerretv heret os.

One steamy afternoon outside Tulsa, my step-cousin Gracie Halfmoon took me to Sonic Drive-In, and we sucked down blue coconut slushes at an outdoor table. I asked, "Who's that?"

Gracie's a Cherokee-Seminole and a total social butterfly. She knows everybody and has lived two blocks from there her entire life.

But before she could reply, the handsome new arrival was offering me a business card. "Thomas Dale Brown, at your service."

The card read *TDB III Productions—independent films.*

He joked, "Baby, I can make you a star."

He had an athletic build, but there was obviously more to this boy than football and fantasizing about future frat parties. I was feeling starry already.

"Sorry, Tommy," Gracie said, squelching the sparks between us. "She's driving back to Kansas tomorrow."

Was he already in a relationship? Was he not into romance? Or was it something else? Gracie didn't seem to like the idea of Tommy and me together, and I trusted her.

As we climbed into Gracie's pickup truck, I felt a little buzzed from the sugary drink and banter. I'd been home long enough for the rhythm in my speech to down-shift. I held myself looser, joked more freely, and shook off the stress that sometimes boiled up in my suburban good-girl mode. There, I could speak my mind and be understood. "How're Tommy's movies?"

"Moody. Thought provoking. He's won a few awards."

Gracie lowered the truck windows and cranked the air conditioner. "Listen, I like the guy. Everybody does. He's one good-looking, smooth-talking Choctaw boy. Talented, hardworking, funny as hell."

We passed a billboard for Creek Nation Casino in nearby Muskogee. "And the catch is?"

"Tommy Dale lives to flirt, and he's good at it. But, for serious, he only dates white girls. Blondes and redheads, for the most part."

Gracie turned up an old Rita Coolidge song on the radio. "Likes 'em movie-star beautiful, I suppose."

A Higher Power

Towering sunflowers strained against barbed wire. Distant thunder rumbled, and on a cloudy, gray afternoon in early August, I ran out of gas on a two-lane Kansas highway. I'd seen the warning light on the dash but forgotten about it, singing along to Beyoncé on satellite radio.

It was only a twenty-minute walk to the nearest station.

I took off on foot, glancing at the splotchy brown cows on one side of the road, the gold-crested green cornfield on the other.

An approaching sedan slowed, and a semifamiliar face leaned out the window. His blond hair blowing in the wind, the driver called, "Louise! Louise Wolfe! Need a ride?"

It was Peter Ney from Immanuel Baptist, the pastor's teenage son. He was going into his junior year at EHHS and was on the Wrestling team.

My family's on-again, off-again search for a new church home had been temporarily derailed by summer travel and my daddy's conviction that anyone who works Saturdays should be forgiven for sleeping in on Sunday mornings. (Never mind that most churches offer a weekly evening service.)

Immanuel Baptist wasn't a contender, though. We'd given it a try, but my family longed for a closer-knit congregation. The idea that we could come and go without seeing anyone we knew seemed to miss the point, and as Mama had pointed out, my brother and I already went to high school with almost two thousand students. We didn't need a thirty-five-hundred-member church, too.

"Out of gas," I admitted, gesturing with a thumb back toward the Honda. "But the nearest station is only—" A flash of lightning caught my eye.

"Get in," Peter said. "I'll give you a ride."

Opening the car door, I felt the first raindrops.

"I have a confession," he added moments later, flicking on his windshield wipers. "I asked around about you, after your family visited Immanuel."

"You did?" I gave Peter a second look. So what if he was a year younger? He had made a positive impression from the start. He'd complimented Mama's King Ranch casserole at the "Welcome Summer" potluck on the church lawn, and over the past few months, he'd sent me a few personal e-mails about upcoming youth activities.

Just because his church wasn't a fit for my family didn't mean he couldn't be a fit for me.

"Hey, I know *you're* a Cam Ryan fan," Peter said. He began chatting nonstop about my ex-boyfriend's football skills and stats.

No doubt Peter had seen Cam and me together last spring and assumed we were still a couple. I probably should've cleared that up then, but I didn't feel like getting into it.

Besides, his being a die-hard fan of Cam Ryan was a major turnoff.

At the Phillips 66, I could barely make out the digital instructions on the narrow, rain-splattered screen displays. But the signage read PLEASE PAY BEFORE PUMPING.

Peter offered to fill the gas can from his trunk while I ran inside.

Overhead fluorescent lights flickered in the station food mart. Hot dogs rotated under a heat lamp. The displays behind the counter hawked lottery tickets, chewing tobacco, and cigarettes. I was signing off on the charge when Peter, dripping, wrenched open the heavy glass door. "Ready?"

"I heard about you and Cam Ryan," the cashier cut in, and on second glance, I recognized him from school. Dylan Something-or-Other. A senior in Debate and wannabe A-lister who routinely traded gossip for social leverage. "Is this your new boyfriend?"

"We're church friends," I replied. A safe enough answer. Downright wholesome.

On the return drive, Peter and I listened to the wipers. Traffic was light. The rain had quieted to a mist. I decided to just say it. "Cam and I broke up."

"I'm not one of the popular people," Peter said, evidently mortified. "I didn't realize . . . You're seniors. I'm only a junior." He raked wet hair off his forehead. "I mean, I'm not a loser. I'm an athlete. I wrestle." That last bit had radiated insecurity.

He added, "I should've asked you before going on and on—"

"No, no," I assured him as a tractor rumbled by. "I should've said something earlier. Cam and I broke up after prom, not long before school let out for summer. It's such a busy time, end of the year and all. I'm sure a lot of people missed it."

Not any of the "popular people," though. They lived for that sort of thing.

But, thinking it over, didn't Peter's cluelessness make him more appealing? Especially given my resolve, socially speaking, to make a fresh start? He was cute and apparently tenderhearted.

"Mind if I ask what went wrong?" Peter nudged. "You two were always hanging all over each other. I was looking forward to bragging that I'd rescued the future homecoming queen."

Just like that, my patience ran out. "Kind of a personal question, don't you think?"

Sunflowers bowed in the wind. Cattle huddled beneath an elm tree for shelter.

22

The rain had intensified again. The thunder had become more demanding.

Peter made a U-turn and parked alongside the country highway behind my mama's Honda Fit. He opened his car door. "I'm already drenched. Let me fuel up—"

"One condition," I said, forcing a smile. "I'll treat you to lunch afterward."

By midafternoon, the crowd at the Grub Pub was sparse and probably wouldn't pick up until happy hour. Nobody was playing pool or darts. I waved at Shelby and chose a leather booth with a view of Sunflower Tea Shop and Antiques. After I introduced her to Peter, she announced, "Some woman just tipped me twelve percent and a button." She showed it to us. "A button?"

I didn't mention that was probably the customer's snide way of commenting on Shelby's low neckline. My mama's old-fashioned enough that she wouldn't let me out of the house looking like that. Shelby's mama had run off with a trucker a couple of years back, and they'd started a new family outside of Lincoln, Nebraska.

Peter blinked at Shelby's cleavage and excused himself to dry off in the restroom.

"What's with Prince Valiant?" she asked once he was gone.

"Out of gas. Weather. Knight in shining sedan." I'd begun to wonder if Peter had asked around about me because he'd been romantically interested but then had backed off after he heard I had a boyfriend. An intimidating, possessive boyfriend. "So far, he's not without potential."

I thought he might be too churchy, though. (I hail from the judge-not school of Protestantism.) Or maybe he was one of those infamously rebellious preacher's kids, and that day's rescue mission had been less about doing unto others and more about doing me.

Shelby extracted a pen from the thick twist of her auburn hair, and I requested two plates of dry-rub wings. As she left to put in the order, I kicked off my soggy sandals and decided to proceed with caution. If I made any more epic mistakes when it came to boys, I wanted them to be of the sparkling new variety. If Peter had issues with Native people, for example, I wanted to know well before I fell for him. As in before our first date.

After he returned to the table, we made small talk about the planned Immanuel Baptist expansion. They were building new classrooms and offices. The project would cost tens of millions, and Peter was feeling weary of heading up one teen-group fund-raiser after another.

"Sorry I snapped at you for asking about me and Cam." Not that I owed Peter an explanation, but I could've been more gracious. "We had a difference of opinion about his older brother's engagement. Cam's future sister-in-law is a Kickapoo woman."

Peter dunked a plump wing into ranch dressing. "You mean, she's a *Native American*? Isn't that the PC thing to say?"

I'd meant "Kickapoo." Maybe it was Peter's way of trying, though. "Cam's mother, she has a problem with the whole mixed-marriage thing. I'm a romantic, and, well, let's just say I could've kept my thoughts to myself." Technically the truth, though I'd left a *lot* out.

Peter pushed away his plate of decimated chicken bones. "That sucks."

He began cleaning his fingers with a Wet-Nap. "Too bad they don't go to Immanuel. My dad does a lot of family counseling, and he always says officiating weddings is his favorite part of the job."

That had sounded like a winning answer until Peter concluded, "And we host weekly AA meetings in the church conference rooms, too."

Toward the end of her waitressing shift, Shelby asked the manager if I could help clear off a ten-top so we could cut out sooner. Rinsing dirty plates in the cramped, messy kitchen, she asked, "You're sure that Peter wasn't talking about Mrs. Ryan?"

I was starting to wish I hadn't mentioned it. "Pretty sure."

"Because Peter did you a solid today and he was all goo-goo eyes and, let's face it, Cam's mother? Known to tip a few. Plus, Louise, you know how much I love you. But you overthink everything in that giant brain of yours, and you can be sensitive. It's what makes you such a great friend, but sometimes . . ."

The air was hot, stuffy, and greasy. I loved the pub, but it was a wonder the health inspector hadn't shut the place down. I loaded glassware into the dishwasher. "Sometimes what?"

The cook, Karl, was a friendly, scruffy white guy with a prominent belly. He lowered a metal basket of waffle fries into the bubbling oil. "Give the guy a break—he was just being honest. A lot of Indians are alcoholics." He raised his voice. "Hell, a lot of *people* are alcoholics. I'm proudly two years sober, little girl—doesn't make me a horrible human being."

A Star Is Born

Outside the men's dressing room, my little brother modeled a pair of dark-wash Levi's.

"Better," I said. "We should pick up a couple of belts. A brown one and a black one."

This was the week before high school started. Twice Mama had taken Hughie clothes shopping and come home empty-handed because, at the last minute, they'd caught a summer blockbuster flick instead.

Basically, Mama felt guilty about the time she had to devote to earning her JD and MA in Indigenous Studies. And Hughie liked watching superhero movies better than trying stuff on.

I'd decided to make it my business. That fall, Hughie and I would be on the same campus for the first time since elementary, but it's not like we'd see each other most of the day.

From what I could tell, he hadn't made any close friends at middle school last semester. Over the summer, he'd bonded with the kids at the nearby American Indian Youth Summer Camp (focused on science and technology), but they all lived in the next town east of us.

Ensuring Hughie's clothes weren't bully bait was one way for me to look out for him.

He gave himself the once-over in the full-length three-panel mirror. "Shoes?"

My brother, who is not especially athletic, has an irrational love of athletic footwear.

"Shoes," I promised.

Hughie changed back into his cargo shorts, and we waited in line to check out behind a couple of accounting students shopping for suits and talking about their job search.

I tried to imagine Hughie as an accountant. It seemed like a career well suited to a quiet, reserved person, and Hughie's best subject is math.

"I signed up for the school newspaper," I reminded him. "That's a class, but it's kind of social, too." Trying not to sound too much like Mama, I added, "Have you thought about getting involved in any school activities?"

"You worry too much." Hughie shook his head. "I never should've told you about those jerks in Cedar Park. You can relax now, Lou. I've got it all figured it out."

Stepping to the sales counter, I reached into my bead-accented purse for my debit card.

As the clerk rang up our purchases, I said, "Okay,

fill me in. What's the Hughie Wolfe personal strategy for high-school success?" I looked up—yes, *up*—at my baby brother under the fluorescent lights. When had he grown taller than me? *"What?"*

Hughie quickly raised and lowered his eyebrows, relishing the suspense.

We exited the department store into the bustling outdoor mall, and he paused at a kiosk of Kansas-themed gifts. As in Kansas Jayhawks, Kansas State Wildcats, sunflowers, and *The Wizard of Oz* movie merchandise, the latter manifesting in snow globes, magnets, key chains, wineglasses, music boxes, and utterly darling ruby-slipper earrings.

My shy, left-brained brother held up a holiday ornament of the Tin Man's head like it was a trophy. "I'm auditioning for the fall musical," Hughie announced. *"The Wizard of Oz."*

Déjà Who?

Hughie and I bounded off the school bus on the sunny first day of our respective freshman and senior years. New and returning students jostled, gossiped, hugged, and moseyed on inside. I overheard cooing over new outfits and snippets about family travel. A voice exclaimed, "I missed you!" Another: "What's up, bro?" Another: "Oh, my God, she's such a slut!"

As we passed the eight-foot-tall Honeybee statue, Hughie warned, "Cam, two o'clock."

All 135 pounds of my brother bristled at the sight of my alpha-jock ex-boyfriend, who was artfully slouching against the brick wall like he was posing for a men's fashion catalog.

"No worries," I told my brother. "He's just waiting for someone."

Turned out that someone was me. "Lou, over here!"

I'd already decided to make a point of saying howdy to him. The way I had it figured, my day-to-day life would require a lot less effort if Cam and I were on friendlier terms.

Besides, I'd done the rejecting, which arguably made him the injured party. And he was making an effort. Publicly.

"Are you getting back together with him?" Hughie asked.

"Lou, please!" Cam called again.

Please? "Not the plan," I assured my brother. "Have a great day!"

I watched Hughie disappear through the formidable front doors and smoothed my wavy hair, which—given the humidity—was already a lost cause.

Didn't matter. I may not be movie-star beautiful, but I'm solidly girl-next-door cute. Hourglassy with muscular legs and the gleaming smile of a dentist's daughter.

That said, Cam and I still had a history. I didn't want to think about how many girls he'd hooked up with over the summer. It wasn't that I wanted him back or wanted him to eat his heart out, but I had my pride. I didn't want him to take one look at me and wonder what he'd ever been thinking, either.

We hadn't run into each other all summer. We hadn't spoken since he'd read my breakup e-mail and told me to "fuck off" last spring in the junior hall.

I strolled over like it was no big deal.

"I missed you," Cam said, pulling me into his arms.

"Loulou, no one knows me like you. There's nobody I can talk to the same way."

The hug, no, the vulnerability in his voice, caught me off guard. I opened my mouth to say I wasn't sure what, and Cam kissed me like we'd never broken up. His tongue claimed mine. His hands slid to grip my behind. We'd had our share of PDAs, but nothing like that.

I shoved him away. "What the hell do you think you're doing?"

"What now?" Cam countered. "Fuck, Louise. I can't do anything right, can I?"

I left him there with his back against the brick wall.

At lunch, Shelby ambushed me entering the chaotic cafeteria. "I knew I should've driven you and Hughie to school," she said. "Clearly, you can't be trusted any-where near Cam Ryan without a personal bodyguard who's immune to his bullshit."

"I didn't kiss him," I clarified, making my way to the food-service line. "He kissed me. There's a difference. And he had no business kissing me."

She gestured to the loud, unruly jocks' table. "You're not sitting with them now?"

Hadn't I made myself clear?

"No," I assured her. "I'm sitting with you."

Hello and Good Bylines

I don't remember noticing Joey that first day in AP Government. I was preoccupied, contemplating Hughie's latest text that EHHS was "the best school ever."

It was during my second class with Joey—Journalism, the last hour on my schedule—that he tossed his canvas shoulder bag to the far side, slid into the desk next to mine, and introduced himself: "Joseph A. Kairouz. Nice to meet you."

"Ambitious use of the power initial," I replied.

"I go by Joey," he added. Clear blue eyes. Sandy brown hair. A cleft in his angular chin.

He carried himself like he was busy, even though he wasn't doing a damn thing.

I didn't realize right off that he was a new student. It's a big school. There were a lot of people I didn't know. "I've never met a Kairouz before."

"It's from the Lebanese side of the family," he said. "My dad's side. Mom's white bread by way of Scotland."

I was more intrigued by the slightly arrogant way he held his lips. "I'm Louise M. Wolfe." I liked the sound of it—mature, accomplished. It would serve as my byline. "Lou."

I could've said something then about being a Creek girl. It would've flowed from the conversation. Would've saved me a lot of heartache and drama, but I was too busy flirting.

Joey's full lips twitched. "M?"

"Melba," I replied. "Like the toast."

"Never heard of it."

It's a family name, like Louise. My great-grandma Melba grew up at Seneca Indian School. She went on to become a nurse during World War II.

"Your loss," I said. "It's crunchy, delicious toast."

The bell rang, and our perky, thirty-something teacher launched into her welcome speech.

"We're the engine of communication here at East Hannesburg High," Ms. Wilson began. "Face-to-face and digital." She mentioned writing, shooting, editing, and deadlines. She waxed poetic about problem solving, ethics, and managing stress. She emphasized that each of us would be required to contribute at least one editorial—aka opinion piece—by the end of the semester.

"We specialize in story—story is what defines us, what brings people together. This class will introduce you to hundreds of people and their stories, and give you the opportunity to share those stories. It will grow your humanity and prepare you to be the heroes of your own lives."

Shades of *Dead Poets Society, The Great Debaters, Mr. Holland's Opus,* and *To Sir, with Love.* I wasn't the only one who'd seen too many of those inspiring-teacher movies.

Still, I liked Ms. Wilson. Her hot-pink cat's-eye glasses and her short gold curls and how she talked so fast, with her voice and hands both.

The *Hive's* staff would be made up of four writers (Joey, me, Emily, Alexis) and a copy editor (Nick), who also drew editorial cartoons and designed infographics.

I recognized Nick. It wasn't just that he's one of two students who uses a wheelchair. He's the campus DJ, too. And we had French class together.

Our intrepid leaders were a managing editor, Daniel, and an editor in chief, Karishma.

Daniel's a top wrestler, best known for tooling around in his dad's classic red Porsche convertible. (The family owns a car dealership.)

Karishma had run for Stu-Co president and lost, but I'd voted for her. We were in many of the same AP classes. Unlike a lot of girls, Karishma spoke her mind without apologizing first.

"Over the course of the semester, you'll become a team," Ms. Wilson continued. "Hopefully even a family —"

"What about video reporting, shooting, editing?" Joey had raised his hand but spoke without being called on. "That's what I did at my old school. That and still photos. I'm good at both." And apparently had no qualms about saying so. "I can write, too," he added. "Sort of."

"Big deal." Daniel held up his phone. "Everybody's a photographer. Videographer. Whatever."

"Check last year's results at state," Joey shot back.

Our school is so sports saturated, it took me a moment to realize he was talking about high-school *journalism* contests.

Ms. Wilson pushed up to sit on the front of her desk. "You'd need to coordinate with the other reporters and cover your own stories, too."

"I can handle it," Joey said. After a beat or two, he seemed to realize that he'd jumped in before the teacher was done talking. "Uh, that's all I wanted to say." He paused. "Go ahead."

Ms. Wilson tilted her head, waiting him out.

"Not that you need me to tell you to go ahead," Joey clarified. "I'm just really interested to hear what you have to say." He cleared his throat. "Thanks, ma'am."

"You're quite welcome," she replied.

My mama was an English teacher for twenty years back in Texas. I could read Teacher Brain. Ms. Wilson liked Joey. She thought he'd be a handful but in a good way.

Karishma passed around a sign-up sheet. "If two people want the same beat, Daniel and I will conduct interviews tomorrow."

By the time it got to me, every beat I was interested in — News, Arts/Entertainment, and Features — had been claimed. That left Sports, which I knew would be largely devoted to Cam. I chose Features instead.

I'd have to interview against Joey to get it.

After the final bell, lockers clanged over the billowing chatter. Hughie had texted to say he wouldn't be riding the late bus. He was going to a new friend's house after the info meeting for the musical. Hughie had already made a friend.

"My little brother is a freshman," I muttered to myself in the hall. "This is his first day of high school, and he's already cooler than me."

Over my shoulder, Joey chimed in. "It's my first day here, and I'm cooler, too."

"That's up for debate," I said, glancing at him. Not as tall as Cam, but still hovering around six feet. Broad shoulders. Wide chest. "And where did you come from?"

"Overland Park." It's a mega middle-class KC suburb on the Kansas side of the Kansas-Missouri state line. A lot like Cedar Park or East Hannesburg.

Strolling alongside me, Joey answered the obvious question. "My parents split up. Mom got a job at Hallmark's production center in Lawrence, and I moved with her to East Hannesburg. Dad works for Southwest Airlines, but we're only an hour from KCI Airport."

Heading up the stairs, I chose the safer topic. "Your dad's a pilot? Was he air force?"

"Yes and yes."

"Mine was army. A dentist." We passed the long row of orange lockers lining the senior hall on one side, the windows looking out at the interior courtyard on the other.

I noticed a couple of Dance girls noticing that Joey and I had noticed each other.

"Any brothers or sisters?" I wanted to know.

"Older sister." Joey adjusted the strap of his canvas bag. "You ask a lot of questions. You'll make a good reporter." He paused for dramatic effect. "But Features will be mine."

"Aren't you the optimist?" I replied.

He laughed and gestured at a locker. "This is my stop."

It was my cue to say good-bye and keep walking. I lingered instead.

Joey reached inside his locker for a biography of Ansel Adams from the school library.

He'd stuck a party pic on the inside of the metal door. While Joey was distracted, I studied the image of him in a navy suit, standing behind a slender white girl in a short, lacy violet dress. The magnetic frame had been decorated with puffy neon-purple ink.

A gift, I realized, from his date. His girlfriend?

"You're in my AP Government class," I said, spotting the textbook.

"That's right," Joey said. "I sit two rows to your right, one seat up."

"How specific," I replied. "You know, coming from someone so much cooler."

That scored me a grin. Once he'd packed up, we moved on, side by side, to the intersection of the lobby and the walkway bridge linking one wing of the school to the other. The administrative and nurse's offices, library, and the majority of the classrooms to the east, the multipurpose room, gyms, locker rooms, auditorium, indoor pool, and whatnot to the west.

Joey paused alongside the immense sports-trophy case. "Uh, Lou, do you want to—?"

"I'll see you tomorrow," I said, tempted to get to know him better but erring on the side of caution. Yes, I was already infatuated with Joey. He'd made an intriguing first impression.

But Peter Ney, the last intriguing boy I'd met, had automatically equated all Native people with alcoholics. And Tommy Dale Brown, the next-to-last intriguing boy I'd met, dated only white girls. (The prevailing theory was that Hollywood had warped his mind.)

Besides, I'd chosen the *Hive* as my new place to belong. On staff, Joey was the competition, and it's not like I needed a boyfriend.

Tiger Lily Has Always Been a Hot Mess

I was polishing off my raisin-cinnamon oatmeal when Mama looked up from her laptop at the kitchen table. "Get this," she said. "Yesterday, the Theater teacher sent out a notice mentioning a more inclusive approach, and today there's a parent group objecting to the—and I quote—'color-blind casting' of the school musical. I've received an e-mail addressed to 'Dear Caring Parent,' asking me to write or call the assistant vice principal to complain."

My brother's upcoming audition was the talk of the house. "Color what?" I asked.

"Better to approach it as color-*conscious* casting," Mama explained. "A color-*blind* approach can lead to whitewashing—white actors in blackface, yellowface, redface . . ."

"Like Rooney Mara as Tiger Lily?" I asked.

"This is different," Mama went on. "Color *conscious* means casting actors of color or, in Hughie's case, Native actors, in roles where the race, ethnicity, skin hue of the character doesn't matter to the story. It opens up opportunities, pushes back against the white default."

"Like a Black actress playing Hermione from *Harry Potter*," my brother called, bounding downstairs with his backpack. "Why not?"

"It can also be an artistic choice to send a message," Mama added. "Like in *Hamilton*."

Hughie grabbed a banana from the bunch hanging beneath the cabinets. "Mrs. Q, the faculty director, is new to the job this year. She's shaking things up."

Apparently. So this parent group was lining up against the student actors of color.

Against Hughie.

I rinsed and loaded my cereal bowl into the dishwasher. "Exactly who sent the e-mail?"

"Pastor's wife at Immanuel Baptist," Mama replied.

Immanuel Baptist was Peter's church, which made the pastor's wife his mother.

Worker Bees

Editor in chief Karishma clasped her hands, all business. "Joey. Louise. No matter which of you gets the Features beat, you'll have to work together this semester, so we decided to interview you both at the same time. The *Hive* isn't about winners and losers. We're a team."

She and Daniel shared the power position behind the teacher's desk while Ms. Wilson once again perched on top of it, off to one side this time.

The managing editor tapped his tablet. "With News, Arts/Entertainment, and Sports, the reporters can get a baseline of assignments from the school calendar and go from there.

"Features isn't like that. You'll have to pitch in to cover their overflow, but you've also got to come up with your own story ideas."

Daniel rolled his eyes. "I can't fucking believe nobody wants Sports."

"Language," Ms. Wilson said, as if out of habit.

"We're looking for a self-starter." Karishma stood, strode over to the whiteboard, uncapped a blue marker, wrote our names side by side, and underlined them.

"We're interested in your vision." She poised the marker. "Joey, you go first."

Before he even started talking, she wrote IMAGES under his name and starred it.

Two student desks had been scooted closer, one for each of us.

Joey straightened in his chair. "I've clicked through the past couple of years of the *Hive*. One major problem stands out: it's boring."

He leaned forward. "Except for one issue last fall. There was a front-page story about some parents trying to get the librarian fired and an editorial saying that was bull—uh, BS. But there was no follow-up coverage. Nothing. Crickets. What happened?"

Karishma and Ms. Wilson traded a loaded look.

"The librarian kept her job," the editor in chief said. Using her fingers to make air quotes, she added, "Some 'objectionable' books were locked in the cage behind the circulation desk. You need a signed permission slip to check them out."

"And some 'objectionable' books . . . disappeared," Ms. Wilson added.

"Banned?" I exclaimed. "Which books? Like sexy books or books with f-bombs?"

"According to the article, it sounded like all that and evolution, too," Joey clarified.

The teacher arched a brow. "Officially, the books were checked out and never returned. Officially, rather than replace them, the library budget is going to higher-priority titles."

"There was nothing about all that in the *Hive*," Joey countered.

"The, uh, would-be book banners got to most of the seniors on staff and bullied them into killing the story," Karishma said, enthusiastically scrawling ARCHIVES under his name. (Joey was scoring bonus points for having done his homework.)

Karishma added, "They love making noise, but if anyone disagrees, they don't want to hear about it. Or anyone else to hear about it, either. They don't think it's the student newspaper's place to quote their opposition."

Joey cocked his head. "Nobody's fucking *getting* to *me*."

"Language," Ms. Wilson echoed, sounding impressed. Because he was a badass, too.

"Me neither," I chimed in, annoyed by my obligatory tone.

What were we talking about? Exactly who got to last year's seniors? How?

"Wait a minute!" I exclaimed. "These parents who tried to get the librarian fired, are they the same parents who're complaining about the color-conscious casting of the musical?"

"Now, there's a newsworthy question!" Karishma

replied. "The answer is yes. Emily's already working on it. Arts/Entertainment is her beat. But good journalistic instincts!"

She added a star to my list and a smiley face, too.

Which may not sound like a huge deal, but it was infinitely gratifying.

Karishma was the only returning staff member. She had recruited everyone except Joey, who'd signed up on his own, and she was looking at him like he was a prize-winning lottery ticket.

But Features is more of a *writer's* writing assignment, isn't it? Less formulaic than News or Sports, more about the captivating lead than the inverted pyramid.

Karishma had heard me read a couple of my essays in AP Lit last spring. She'd mentioned my writing ability when she urged me to sign up for the *Hive*.

She had to know I was the best reporter for the job.

"Joey, why don't you want Sports?" I asked. Obnoxious of me, I know. But most boys hardly talk about anything else, and Joey looked athletic.

"Why don't *you* want Sports?" he countered.

Ms. Wilson had crossed the room and stepped up on a chair to tack up a First Amendment poster between a laminated front page from the Kansas City Royals' last World Series win and a laminated front page from the last KU NCAA basketball championship.

"What if we expand Features?" she suggested, hopping down. "Lou and Joey can work together and separately. It'll give Joey plenty of room to make the *Hive* less boring." She shook her blond curls. "That comment really stung."

(Yes, teacher humor at its finest.)

"I like it," Karishma said. "Joey will be too busy shooting for everyone else to cover a whole beat by himself." She capped her marker. "Daniel, how about you take Sports?"

Made sense to me. Daniel's a quintessential jock—always in his letterman jacket and class ring. He's like Cam that way, except just shy of a foot shorter.

"What about Wrestling?" Nick called from the back, copyediting at his desk near the equipment-storage cabinet. "Daniel can't cover his own meets."

Alexis, the News reporter, had just returned from the restroom. "I'll take it. I have an older brother who wrestled. The coach loved him."

(The first meet isn't until December anyway.)

"Can I be the managing editor and the Sports reporter?" Daniel asked Ms. Wilson.

"I don't know," she replied, proudly surveying her journalistic wall display. "Can you?"

Daniel pumped his fist into the air. "Hell, yeah!"

Fledgling in Flight

Inspired by Hughie's middle-school experience, I pitched the editors a story on bullying. "The *Hive* has tackled the topic before," I admitted. "But not within the past three years, and the bulk of our student readership has turned over since then."

(Joey wasn't the only one who could check the archives.)

"That's a fairly ambitious feature for your first week," Karishma mused. She and Daniel were seated across from each other, as if for dueling keyboards. "It's already Wednesday."

They were working on a joint editorial about the importance of free discourse in student media. Karishma had scribbled her ideas on purple Post-it notes. He'd jotted his on blue ones, and they kept moving them around the tabletop. From their bickering, I could tell it wasn't going well.

"I am ambitious," I replied. "I'd like to make a difference for students who—"

"Blah, blah, blah," Joey said, coordinating his videography schedule with Alexis's calendar of school events. Three long tables had been positioned, parallel, behind the two rows of single desks up front. He and Alexis had set up in the middle of the room.

Was he mocking me or waving off distant assignments?

"As I was saying," I tried again, "I'd like to make a difference, but I'd appreciate any tips on identifying sources." I hated being high-maintenance, but I was still booting my post-Cam social presence. And, if I wanted to make Friday's back-to-school issue, my article had to be in to Nick for copyediting by early that morning.

Daniel snagged one of Karishma's purple Post-it notes and scribbled *Wyatt Hanley* on it.

"Friend of yours?" I asked, sticking it inside my Journalism binder.

The managing editor shrugged. "Some of the guys give him a hard time."

"Some of the guys?" Karishma nudged.

"I didn't do anything!" Daniel exclaimed. "I can't control my friends."

"You could talk to them," I pointed out.

"Sure, gang up on me." He stood from the table. "Wyatt rides a neon-green mountain bike to school. Should be locked out front. You can't miss it."

With that, Daniel began crumbling up a few of his own sticky notes, tossing them like basketballs toward the trash can.

Karishma ignored him. "Bullying . . . Lou, it's a huge topic, complicated, sensitive. I want you to go after big stories this year. But right now, you're a brand-new reporter."

"Give me a chance," I said. "Let me show what I can do."

She steepled her fingers. "Okay. Let's see how it goes and . . . if you need a backup idea, you might consider doing a feature on the new head janitor."

"Sounds thrilling," I muttered, discouraged by her lack of faith.

The bell rang. As I was hurrying past the teacher's desk to beat Wyatt to the bike rack, Ms. Wilson said, "About the new custodian . . . last year, the cafeteria staff compiled a top-twenty list of all the rude, crude things that students had said to them. It was kind of funny and kind of not funny. Some kids treat certain staff members like they're invisible or, worse, beneath them."

Ms. Wilson began cleaning her glasses. "Some teachers and administrators do, too."

I hadn't thought about it like that.

Wyatt was a senior of average height and weight. He had a generic short haircut and dressed to blend. The only remarkable things about him were his lime-green bicycle and how much he didn't want to talk to me.

"Who put you up to this?" he asked, opening the bike lock. "Cam Ryan?"

"No." Mentioning Daniel seemed like a bad idea. "I told you. I'm here for the *Hive.* Karishma Sawker is the editor in chief. I'm doing a story about bullying."

Wyatt was still scanning the waves of departing students. "How did my name come up?"

"I'm interviewing several people." I hoped to, anyway. "Do you have anything to say?"

Gripping the handlebars, he replied, "I don't want you to use my name."

I could call him "unidentified senior." I suggested, "Off the record, then?"

"Off the record," Wyatt echoed. "I hate school. I hate the halls. I hate the cafeteria. I hate the locker room and the restrooms and the goddamn bus."

He straddled his bike. "I hate every asswipe who messes with me and everybody who laughs when they do. I hate how the Gym teachers look away, especially the ones who coach. How they protect the Cam Ryans of the world. Most of all, I hate girls who go for guys like him." Ouch. Hard not to take that one personally.

As Wyatt pedaled off, I keyed the quote into my phone as fast as I could.

Thursday morning, I struck out with the counselor's office.

The school secretary said, "I'm sure that Mrs. Evans has plenty of helpful materials. After all, we have zero tolerance for bullying."

However, it was too late to get an interview appointment for that same day, and Ms. Wilson had cautioned us against "regurgitating information" from the Internet.

Coming out of Calc, I heard a sneering feminine voice say, "Nice outfit, Paul Bunyan."

The target was Sage Schmidt, who's tall and robust and sported faded overalls with a square-cut white T and hiking boots. Sage lives in Emerald Hills, my subdivision, and we'd chatted once at our neighborhood pool. "You okay?" I asked.

Sage's wry smile surprised me. "I can Bunyan with the best of them. All I need is a blue ox, and, hey, who doesn't want a blue ox?"

"I'd love a blue ox," I agreed. Then Sage filled me in on how the name-caller had been routinely picked on by other girls back in elementary school.

"Sorry, Lou." Karishma glanced up from my draft. "We can't do anything with this for Friday. You only have two sources, and one of them is anonymous. And you reported just one side of the incident you witnessed in the hall."

"The other side said, 'No comment.'"

More like, "Go to hell," but somehow, I didn't think that would fly in the *Hive*.

"We're a school paper," Karishma replied. "We've got to protect our credibility. There's too much editorializing, overgeneralizing. We'd need to hear from an expert and include resources—"

"Got it," I replied, reaching for my notebook. "Can we finish this tomorrow?"

Preferably when Joey wasn't smirking while Nick copyedited his already approved story on a junior who was raising three rescued crow chicks. (And of course, Joey had video to boot.)

"It's nothing personal," Karishma assured me. "You're not the only one struggling with an assignment."

True. Auditions for the musical had been "temporarily" put on hold, and neither the faculty director nor the administration was willing to talk to Emily about it.

"I'm not upset," I replied. Not exactly, and I wasn't going to miss out on a byline in the first issue. "Can we talk more later? I have a janitor to track down and only twenty-two minutes before the final bell."

Story Circle

On Labor Day, after a hearty breakfast of Texas-shaped waffles, Mama and I did homework and drank sweet tea at our antique kitchen table.

For her, pursuing a law degree and a master's in Indigenous Studies was a huge adjustment. She'd shifted from teacher to student, quit her Tuesday-night book club, and stored her beading supplies on our laundry-room shelf. To me, the new normal didn't feel much different from the countless previous times I'd studied while she graded English papers.

I reviewed a diagram of the skin (epidermis, dermis, hypodermis) for AP Anatomy and Physiology. Meanwhile, she turned a page in her Civil Procedure textbook, muttering, "Rituals, code words, posturing."

"Posturing?" I echoed. "They teach ego at KU Law?"

"No need," she replied. "Plenty to go around already, although I suppose that's true of every law school and a great deal of legal practice, too."

I suspected she needed a pep talk. "You're becoming a lawyer"—and then I quoted Mama's words back to her—"'to defend tribal sovereignty and to keep American Indian children in American Indian families and communities,' where we belong."

She chuckled. "You're a good listener."

"Yes," I agreed. "Yes, I am."

Mama turned another page. "I may need to hear you repeat that every so often."

"Yes," I replied, like a vow. "Yes, I know."

The college application process is like a part-time job unto itself. Karishma's and Nick's families were among those who'd hired professional consultants.

Mine was more of an in-house effort. The University of Kansas was my top choice, and I would have no trouble meeting the assured admissions criteria. Consequently my focus was less about where to go than how to cover the costs, especially since Mama and I would both be paying tuition for two overlapping years, and Hughie and I for at least one.

Mama had briefly set aside her studies to review one of my scholarship essays, reflecting on the protests we'd attended over the years in Austin, Oklahoma City, and Topeka.

"Maybe it would be better to pick one and go deep,"

she suggested, seated across from me. "Tie it into your newfound interest in the news media."

"It's not like I've decided to major in journalism or communications," I said.

Not yet, anyway. I'd been a co-reporter on Features for over a week, and so far, my one contribution to the *Hive* had been the personality profile on the new head custodian. (He'd grown up in Wichita and ran a hot-air balloon business on the side.)

The doorbell rang. "It's 'Joey'?" Mama asked, standing.

"Joseph A. Kairouz," I reminded her. "We're doing a story today for the *Hive*."

Meanwhile Daddy had been coming in through the sliding-glass back door. "A newspaper with no paper involved."

"Better for the trees," Mama pointed out. "Reduces litter."

"The *Hive* sounds like an evil space empire," Hughie said, following Daddy inside, scripts in hand. They'd been running lines on the deck. "Do y'all buzz to the will of your queen?"

I had a sudden flash of Karishma in the Honeybees mascot costume. "Pretty much."

"Oh, how I love air-conditioning," Daddy said, pouring himself a tall glass of iced tea. "When is Lou's new boyfriend supposed to arrive?"

"He's not my boyfriend," I said, not for the first time.

"That's probably him at the front door now," Mama announced.

I could tell Joey would be treated to a Wolfe family welcome.

We'd gone through a similar ordeal the first time Cam had picked me up.

That in mind, I got up and strolled across the great room to the mesquite coffee table. Sure enough, Daddy had strategically fanned out his gun and hunting enthusiast magazines, his military and veteran magazines.

I held one up. "Please tell me you're not using these as a warning to Joey."

"You are my only daughter." Daddy squared his chin, caught in the act. "Hughie's my only son. I have every intention of instilling a healthy respect in his future dates, too."

Mama moved to gather up the magazine display. "We can't always be looking over their shoulders," she said. "We have to trust them to make smart choices."

"They're not the ones I don't trust," Daddy replied, slicing a lemon. "I remember what it was like to be a teenager."

"This isn't even a date situation!" I exclaimed. "Joey is a classmate. We've got a Journalism assignment. We're going to be working together a lot this semester. Platonically."

When Daddy shrugged, I finally caught on that he was just messing with me.

Mama realized it at the same time. "You're incorrigible," she said.

Pleased with himself, Daddy took a sip of tea. "I try."

Goofball. I put in, "By the way, Joey's father is a vet, too—air force."

Hughie, bouncy with thespian energy, gestured toward the foyer. "Do you want me to let him in or should we leave him out on the front step all day?"

The doorbell rang again.

Once Joey had been given the friendly once-over, we headed out to his white hardtop Jeep Wrangler. It was slightly dented, had four doors and tinted windows, and appeared to have been newly washed.

"Careful getting in," Joey said, opening the door for me. "There's a problem with the floorboard on the passenger side."

I looked down, all the way to the concrete. "*What* floorboard on the passenger side?"

As I climbed in, my balance wavered and then I briefly felt Joey's strong, steadying hands against my back. "I've got it," I assured him, half turning to position myself.

"Tuck your legs up on the seat," Joey suggested.

I took his advice and fastened my seat belt. "We're going to the mall?"

"You say that like you don't like malls."

I don't dislike them exactly. Joey hadn't spelled out his story idea, only that he wanted me to partner with him on it. He came around the vehicle and joined me inside.

"Why didn't you want Sports?" I asked in a far more pleasant tone than I'd used in the newsroom. "It's the most-clicked page on the *Hive*."

"I did want Sports," he replied, which made no sense at all.

Backing out of my driveway, Joey added, "I was overthinking, obsessing." Making his way down the cul-de-sac, he explained, "It's my ex-girlfriend. We started going out in ninth."

"The girl in the picture in your locker?"

As a lawn-care truck cruised by, I realized I'd been too quick to fill in the blank.

Joey turned onto the sugar-maple-lined avenue. "Pathetic, right? I should take it down."

He winced. "Last spring, she hooked up with my best friend." His grip tightened on the steering wheel. "I caught them . . . at a house party. On the trampoline."

Yowza. From what I'd gathered, that must've fallen somewhere near the end of his parents' divorce. Bad timing. Apocalyptic.

We passed the Emerald Hills community clubhouse and swimming pool on the left, four model homes on the right. Signs on both sides read OPEN HOUSE, and the subdivision entrance was landscaped in boulders, red hollyhocks, and ornamental grasses.

"You don't want to run into your ex and her, uh, boyfriend at the games?"

Joey had mentioned that he'd gone to West Overland High School, and the West Overland teams were on the EHHS sports schedules. Either his emotional wound was still too fresh or Joey had thought the distraction would keep him from doing his best work. Maybe both.

The silence in the Jeep was palpable until we'd almost reached our destination.

Finally I said, "Maybe they won't show—"

"He's a yell leader," Joey told me. "She's in Marching Band."

He took the mall exit. "They'll be there. I'll be doing a ton of visual and overflow Sports coverage regardless, but I didn't want to be obligated to go to every game. Daniel will just have to make do without me for that one."

"'Big deal,'" I said, quoting the managing editor in the newsroom, day one. "'Everybody's a photographer. Videographer. Whatever.'"

Joey winked at me.

When we arrived at Burnham Outlets, the parking lot was full, so Joey pulled his Jeep into the concrete garage. The three aboveground levels were likewise packed, but we scored one of the few remaining spots in the basement.

The mall is home to national retail shops, chain restaurants, a dine-in movie theater, the new city hall, and the main public library.

The walks are paved with gold bricks bearing the names of local library donors.

Walking out with his tripod, Joey said, "The light today is amazing."

Labor Day sales signs filled the storefront windows. Little kids bounced, shrieking, in a colorful ball pit. Yogurt-store clerks on the sidewalk offered free samples.

Gleaming antique cars occupied the main thoroughfare, and a western trio of middle-aged white dudes strummed guitars in the gazebo. Joey's stride was long and purposeful.

"What's our story?" I asked, hurrying to catch up. "Forty percent off electronics?"

Joey gestured toward a long vintage vehicle with formidable tail fins. "That's a 1959 Cadillac limo." Then he pointed to a short, pasty teenage guy with noticeable acne, wearing a backward ball cap. "That's Elijah Krueger. He's a junior at East Hannesburg."

I didn't recognize the face, but we must've passed in the halls.

"He and his grandfather restored the car," Joey went on. "We're talking hundreds of hours of cleaning, rebuilding, installing, painting, polishing. A fair chunk of retirement savings. You ask the questions. I'll shoot the footage."

Questions. "Give me a minute, okay?" I situated myself on a cobalt-blue metal bench, its design mimicking butterfly wings. Then I retrieved a notepad and pen from my purse.

I wrote: *who, what, when, where, how,* and *why.* The whole thing felt much more real than when I'd talked to the janitor at school. I started writing down a question. Crossed it out.

Joey sat next to me, his backpack at his feet. The tripod to one side. The side of his thigh pressed against the side of my thigh. "Watch."

A trim, bearded man in his sixties gave Elijah an ice-cream cone.

Joey said, "That's the grandfather, George."

A young couple with a bright-red balloon tied to their stroller stopped for a closer look at the fancy silver car, and George began pointing out its features.

"Elijah's grandparents first met in San Diego," Joey continued. "His grandmother died last year, two days before Christmas. Heart attack."

How horrible. Grieving would've been hard enough without "Joy to the World" blasting through the air and passersby wishing the family a happy holiday.

I resolved to move up my weekly calls to my own grandmas and grandpas to that very night. I'd be sure to e-mail them new photos of me and Hughie, too.

"Over winter break, Elijah's hoping to take the limo and road-trip with his granddad to San Diego to scatter his grandmother's ashes," Joey said. "His parents aren't keen on him and George splitting the driving."

Newly licensed driver. California highways. My parents would've been skittish, too.

"They've already given me start-to-finish pics of the whole restoration process—I can edit those in later. But we still need conversational video of Elijah and George with the car."

Joey gently elbowed me. "I bet they'll open up more if you're the one asking the questions."

Flattering, but the story was practically finished. I saw zero reason why Joey couldn't have handled the rest by himself. Had he invited me as an excuse to spend time together? Or . . . ?

"You're *training* me, aren't you?"

"And Emily and Alexis." Joey stood, hoisting the tripod. "Karishma will handle Daniel and Nick."

I gaped at him. "Karishma's the big-boss editor. You're not in charge of—"

"I'm the other person on staff who knows what he's doing. She's counting on me, and I don't believe in half-assed work. When we're teaming up, I can't waste energy babysitting you. When you're on your own, I can't have you doing a shitty job for my school newspaper."

His school newspaper?

The Tin Man

The longing yet peppy lyrics of "If I Only Had a Heart" led me to Hughie. His skinny elbows resting on his skinny knees, he'd retreated to the wood-shingle roof on the gentle slope between our bedroom windows. Night insects—crickets, katydids?—droned backup vocals.

I leaned out. "You can sing!" Given that he'd spent his whole life mouthing the "Happy Birthday" song and the words over his hymnals, who knew?

"You're biased." My brother was stargazing through binoculars. "Yvhiketv cvyace tos."

"Of course I'm biased." Not that Hughie would be signing with a major recording label any time soon, but he could caress the notes, evoke the feels. "Does this mean . . . ?"

"Yes!" Hughie exclaimed. "We're finally having auditions tomorrow after school." It was early September, a week after they'd originally been scheduled. "Mrs. Q refused to back down. She says she's the faculty director, and she's in charge of the musical—period."

I was thrilled to hear that was settled. The show would go on.

I joined him on the roof, mindful of my footing. "How's life in the theater?"

"Everyone's so funny." Hughie lowered the binoculars. "Huge personalities."

Before the showbiz bug bit, my brother had been all outer space, all the time. We used to visit NASA's Johnson Space Center in Houston twice a year, and there's an eight-by-ten signed glossy of Chickasaw astronaut John B. Herrington hanging in Hughie's bedroom.

He added, "You should hear this one senior, though. Garrett—Garrett Ferguson. He's all 'You're a freshman. You're supposed to be low man on the totem pole.' He didn't say it mean, but he meant what he said."

Sounded mean to me. "What set him off?"

"The old director—before Mrs. Q—had talked about putting on *Grease* this fall but then he decided to retire. Garrett had figured on landing the lead role of Danny Zuko. Plus he says the best parts in *The Wizard of Oz* are for girls."

We lived near the top of the hill to the south side of the curve of our fourteen-house cul-de-sac. I gazed across Emerald Hills subdivision at the arched streetlights illuminating new-construction homes in one of four floor plans, each painted in one of four neutral color combinations. There's no such thing as neutral when it comes to people.

"This Garrett guy," I began, "I take it he's your competition for the Tin Man?"

Hughie nodded, adding, "Wait until Chelsea lands Dorothy. And she will. You should check out her videos online."

As my brother gushed, I pulled my phone out of my back pocket to do as he'd suggested. Hughie hadn't been exaggerating. Chelsea was a pretty Black girl with a powerhouse voice, a professional singing voice. I hadn't known her name, but I recognized her from school.

"You really like her," I observed. "I can tell by the way you've been going on."

Hughie got quiet. I should've said "admire." She's a senior. He's a freshman. He didn't have a shot, but crushes don't care about reality. Still, I hadn't meant to embarrass him.

"Like you and Joey," Hughie finally replied. "You talk about him all the time."

"I do not," I insisted. At my brother's teasing smile, I added, "It's only that Joey thinks he knows everything, and he doesn't listen to anybody except maybe Karishma. And if he's going to spend all semester lording last year's state awards over the rest of us, I—"

Hughie handed me his binoculars. Hard to see much, what with the light pollution, but my brother's voice lit up the stars. "You do realize that you've just proven my point?"

At 11:12 p.m., I texted Shelby from my bedroom and her face popped up on my screen.

"Do you talk about Joey Kairouz all the time?" She laughed. "No, you just talk about how he's not afraid to share his feelings and likes old farts and veterans and social outcasts and sappy love stories and drives a crappy Jeep, and, oh yeah, you spent an entire evening at the pub trying to guess his middle name—I'm still going with Almanzo."

Joey and I have something else in common, too. How rare we are at our school, in this suburb, at least when it comes to heritage. So far as I knew, Hughie and I were the only Native students. Joey's Lebanese on his dad's side. He might well be the only Arab American.

We didn't fit the majority profile. We didn't fit the minority profile.

The school district counted us as Other.

I didn't want to get into all that with Shelby, though. "I said 'elders,' not 'old farts.' I did not call his Jeep crappy. Aren't *we* social outcasts? Death before Almanzo, and . . . when I was trying to pitch my bullying story, I heard him saying 'Blah, blah, blah.'"

Shelby was cracking up. "Blah, blah, blah. Lou, he's posturing. You can handle him on the *Hive*. You can handle him off the *Hive*. God knows you've dated worse."

She was right. Hughie was right. "I do talk about Joey all the time."

I slid back beneath my puffy sky-blue comforter. "I like him."

Harmony Haven

A freshly microwaved pillow radiated heat into my neck and shoulders as my feet soaked in a copper basin of warm, sea-salted water and *Legally Blonde* played on the overhead screens. It was September 10, aka my eighteenth birthday, and Shelby was treating us with the help of a 60-percent-off Internet coupon. "This place is hilarious," I said. "Thank you."

Likewise positioned, she was holding up bottles of bright turquoise and shimmery lavender polish, trying to decide. "To think you doubted me."

I'd never thought of myself as a nail-salon person, but my best friend might've managed to convert me. The pedicurists raised our feet in turn from the basins and dried them with fluffy white towels. I'd never felt so decadent.

"Let me get this straight," Shelby began. "You gave your family a present for *your* birthday?" She adjusted her neck pillow. "I don't think you understand how the system works."

Little did she know, I'd slipped a eucalyptus bath bomb for Shelby to the checkout clerk.

"You can't argue with the birthday girl." I showed her pics on my phone of the newest members of my family. "They're dachshunds. Bilbo and Frodo."

"Weiner dogs!" Shelby exclaimed. We chatted about the puppies and nibbled blue M&M's as the pedicurists trimmed, buffed, painted, and told us about their own pets.

While our toenails were drying (hers Amethyst Mist, mine Desert Taupe), Shelby asked, "Have you been mad at me?"

At my blank expression, she added, "The only time I see you is at lunch in the cafeteria or at the Grub Pub while I'm waitressing and you're studying."

She also gave me rides to school and we texted, but . . . "You're always working."

"I always need money," Shelby replied. It was a circular argument. With her jam-packed schedule, it was up to me to make time when she was available.

"Can you think of, say, two or three other seniors who work?" I asked. "Or not just seniors. Anybody at our school." Students with jobs never got featured in the *Hive* like the arts, sports, academic, or Stu-Co types.

Shelby gingerly slipped on her flip-flops. "Sure, but why?"

"Story idea," I said. "Shelby Keller, you're newsworthy."

One September Mourning

Mr. McCloud is white, balding, about ten years from retirement, and one of those solid, heavyset guys who became a teacher so he could make a living as a coach, by which I mean, that's what he told us on the first day of class. (He heads up Cross-Country in the fall, Track and Field in the spring.) But he also has a passion for politics.

There had been no moment of silence that morning like at my school in Texas (in fact, we'd had a pep rally), but Mr. McCloud did lecture on 9/11. September 11, 2001.

"Imagine being a passenger on Flight 93," Mr. McCloud said. "Al Qaeda terrorists have hijacked and crashed commercial jets—two into the Twin Towers in New York City and one into the Pentagon in Arlington, Virginia. Would you fight back? Even if it meant crashing into that field in western Pennsylvania?"

The teacher wrote NEARLY 3,000 DEAD on the chalkboard and circled it.

"What are the values that define our country?"

His gaze weighed the room. "What does the word *patriot* mean to you?"

I thought of Daddy, how he'd served in the army in Iraq. After he was discharged, a dental-school classmate invited him to join her practice in nearby Olathe. He was still adjusting to civilian life, family life. I remembered Joey saying that his father had served in the air force. Of the people in our class, were we the only two from military families?

"As a generation, you're about to inherit a nation, a world, plagued by terrorism and bigotry," Mr. McCloud said. "Here in the States, we've seen a rise in Islamophobia, loathsome political discourse, and hate crimes directed at Arabs, Muslims, Jews, and immigrants, especially refugees. What are *you* going to do about it?"

"Easy," replied Brandon Delaney, the vice principal's son. "We nuke the hell out of the entire Middle East. Turn it into a parking lot." He held out his hands as if to say *ta-da*. "Kill every last one of those fuc—terrorists. Problem solved."

"While also killing millions of innocent people?" Karishma asked. She's one of the few brown students at school. I appreciated her speaking up. I wondered what her religion was.

"Better them than us." Brandon's tone suggested that he meant better *you* than us.

Suddenly hyperaware of his Lebanese heritage, I glanced at Joey. Two rows to my right, one seat up. He'd clenched his jaw and fisted his hands on his desk.

I couldn't help thinking of how I'd felt on those few occasions when Native history came up in a class. Or didn't when it should've.

Frustrated, nauseated. Torn between wanting to talk back and wanting to disappear.

Mr. McCloud moved to stand directly in front of Brandon. "Have you put any thought into white Christian-American terrorism?"

"No," Brandon replied. "Because that's not a thing. You hear the word *terrorism* and what always comes next is a Muslim name." Other kids were nodding.

"The Klan's not a thing?" Joey countered. It was the first time he'd ever spoken in class. "The KKK is a white Christian-American terrorist group."

He'd taken his time enunciating those last five words.

"And there's what happened in Oklahoma City," I put in. April 19, 1995. The Murrah Federal Building, a truck bomb: 168 lives lost, including 19 kids.

I'd visited the memorial with my family the previous summer.

"What about Oklahoma City?" Brandon wanted to know.

Mr. McCloud rested his knuckles on Brandon's desktop. "Show me your phone."

"I wasn't using it," he protested.

"Didn't ask if you were," the teacher replied.

With a sigh, Brandon fished the phone out of his jeans pocket. "Now what?"

"Do a search," Mr. McCloud said. "Read up on the Oklahoma City bombers. Count their Kansas ties, and then decide whether *you* deserve to get nuked for *their* act of terrorism."

The Home Team

Callbacks for the musical were posted outside the auditorium doors that day after school. At my locker, I had my phone in my hand when Hughie's text came in.

Four pizza emojis! (His personal choice for expressing joy.)

He'd be reading again for the role of the Tin Man.

Third quarter, the Harvesters led the Honeybees 14–12. Instead of celebrating with the Theater crowd, Hughie had joined me in soaking up the Friday night lights on the old Hannesburg side of the stadium.

East Hannesburg and old Hannesburg were separate, neighboring towns with schools in the same district. East Hannesburg was new, pricier, generic. Old Hannesburg was heavy on historical charm. Its official name was simply "Hannesburg," but people tended to refer to it as "old Hannesburg" or "old town." Or at least my fellow students at EHHS did.

One of Hughie's Indian Camp buddies, a Leech Lake Band Ojibwe named Dmitri Headbird, was the Harvesters' placekicker.

"I still can't believe it." Hughie couldn't stop talking about the musical. "Can y'all believe it? I might actually get a part."

My phone pinged. Joey. He'd texted *Did you defect?*

Filming from the sidelines, he must've caught sight of me in the bleachers.

On the time-out, Joey directed his lens toward East Hannesburg Varsity Cheer.

From the other side of the field, I couldn't hear the Honeybees squad, but I recognized their moves from pep rallies: "S-T!" *Clap, clap!* "I-N-G!" *Clap, clap, clap!* "Sting! The! Harvesters!" *Clap!*

Back on the field, the quarterback's arm arched. I watched Joey shoot the release and swivel to capture the ball's flight. He zeroed in on the receiver's home jersey—*touchdown!*

The old-town fans, tasting victory, roared to their feet.

Meanwhile, Hughie and Queenie Washington—she's a Black Seminole—had been discussing his audition. She shared that she'd been named after Queen Latifah, and they'd bonded over the magnificence of Queen Latifah as the Wizard in *The Wiz Live!*

I waved at my cousin, Cassidy Rain Berghoff

(technically, she's my second cousin), and Dmitri's twin, Marie, who were climbing the stairs with soft drinks, a bag of popcorn, and what in the Midwest passes for nachos.

I accepted a Diet Coke from Rain and held out my phone to her. "What. Should. I. Say?"

My cousin handed Queenie the nachos and bent to read.

Rain said, "Invite him to meet up with us for pizza."

On the field below, Dmitri positioned himself to kick for the extra point.

Joey didn't meet up with us for pizza. He didn't even bother to reply.

That night, Hughie stayed at the Headbirds' trailer with Dmitri and, across town, I drifted off in my sleeping bag on Rain's bedroom floor.

A tired creak of the old farm-style house awakened me not long after four a.m.

Marie was snoring softly. Queenie had curled on her side, and my cousin had left the room with her black Labrador retriever.

I grabbed my phone, which had been recharging on Rain's hope chest, and checked messages. In the wee hours, Joey had finally texted *Busy editing b-roll.*

Workaholic. I wiggled out of the padded bag and made my way down the ivy-stenciled hallway, past the Trail of Tears painting and the nursery.

Rain's mama died eight years ago, and her daddy is stationed in Guam. So she lives with her big brother,

Fynn; his new wife, Natalie; and their toddler, Aiyana. (It doesn't hurt that her grampa and step-gramma Berghoff live just around the block.)

I'd logged quality time with my cousins the previous summer, tag-team babysitting and helping Fynn with billing and promotional copy for his web-design business.

I found Rain out on the porch swing. "Couldn't sleep?" I asked her.

At her feet, the big dog yawned, and I crouched to scratch his chin.

Rain angled her screen so I could view a selection of her photos. Some in color, some in black and white. Powwow traders, shawl dancers, jingle dancers. The historic downtown, Blue Heaven Trailer Park, and Haskell Indian Nations University in Lawrence.

Family images. Her late mama's tear dress, Aiyana finger-painting, and a selfie of Rain and I cuddling her darling niece at Fynn and Natalie's wedding. At the reception in the church basement, we were the ones who finished off the marble marzipan sheet cake.

Rain and I share Muscogee-Cherokee heritage, and we both have Ojibwe ancestry on the other sides of our families. Her relations are Saginaw Chippewa. Mine are Grand Traverse Band of Ottawa and Chippewa. We're also both descendants of Irish and Scottish immigrants. She's German-American on her dad's side, too.

Rain's photography reflects her hometown, her cultures, the people she cares about most. She has a compelling way of capturing movement, light, emotion.

With stills, she's better than Joey. My cousin occasionally shoots for her small-town paper, the *Hannesburg Weekly Examiner,* partly because her new sister-in-law is the News editor.

When I'd mentioned to Rain that Karishma, the incoming editor in chief of my school paper, had asked me to sign up, my cousin was the one who'd encouraged me most.

Now that the semester was under way, she asked, "How's your journalism class?"

"I need an editorial topic." The *Hive* comes out every Friday, and I was expected to contribute an opinion piece by the end of the semester. "Something that matters. Something—"

"Something that'll beat out Joey's?" Rain teased.

"I refuse to dignify that with an answer." I laughed. "Okay, yes, that would be nice."

I joined her on the porch swing, and my cousin tossed me a crocheted throw.

"What if you did something on how people talk?" she began. "How girls can get called a slut for anything, for nothing, and people will repeat it, too. Post it all over online."

Her tone hinted at personal experience.

My poetic, soft-spoken cousin, who scribbles in journals and reveals stories in shadows. In her whole life, she's kissed only one boy, one time.

Her childhood nickname was Rainbow.

Story Behind the Stories

Dylan Shuster is the debate team captain and a notorious gossip.

He's also a working student. I perched on the bar stool next to his behind the Phillips 66 checkout counter. Joey had already been by to shoot some on-the-job pics.

"Can I have photo approval?" Dylan asked, setting out boxes of candy bars and protein bars next to the cash register.

"You'll have to take that up with Joey and the editors." Using my phone, I opened an app and hit Record. Audio note-taking was a new *Hive* policy in cases where the interview wasn't on video, partly so that the reporters could cross-check to verify our facts and partly so no source could holler about being misquoted. I'd take handwritten notes, too.

Meanwhile, a hefty, fair-skinned man wearing a camouflage windbreaker came in. His matching camo ball cap was pulled low. He'd parked his pickup truck on the far side of the lot, even though all the spots in front were available except the one I'd taken.

"I like to work," Dylan informed me. "I don't see why more students don't work. I mean, you have to *get* a job, and that's not always easy. This is perfect, though, because the owner doesn't care if I do my homework while I'm here. I don't beg my parents for money, and they can't control what I do with what I earn, though I choose to give them half."

There was a lot to unpack in that. Especially the last line, which had felt intentionally wedged into the conversation. "You give them half?" I asked, scribbling what he'd said.

"I'm perfectly capable of contributing to my family," Dylan informed me. "If this was yore, I could've been married with two kids and a blacksmith shop by now."

Was he trying to debate me? "Still, most kids our age don't give money to their parents."

Suddenly Dylan seemed distracted, nervous. "Help yourself if you want a Coke or something," he said, checking the surveillance camera feed of the rear of the store.

The lone customer seemed momentarily torn between cashews and peanuts. Then he opened the mini fridge of fishing bait ($3.22 a cup) and closed it again.

I pushed off the stool and grabbed a zero-calorie orange drink from a fridge.

Dylan explained, "My dad used to manage a sporting-goods shop, but it went out of business. He picks up seasonal work at the home-repair store, but . . ."

I wasn't sure how personal to get. "Is your dad your, um, primary custodial parent?"

"What?" he asked as a pickup truck towing an Airstream pulled up to a pump. "Oh, no, but my mom has to take care of my baby brother and little sisters and my great-grandma."

As I unscrewed the cap on my drink, it struck me that I was writing down a lot of his family's personal business. I didn't think my own parents would want me talking publicly about our finances. "Did you mention to your folks that you were doing this interview for the *Hive*?"

Dylan surveyed the activity outside. A convertible Volkswagen Beetle had also swung in to fuel up. His gaze flicked back to the store camera video. "Did you see him, the guy dressed like a hunter, go into the restroom?"

I shook my head. "I wasn't paying attention."

The brass bell mounted above the door jangled, and I realized it hadn't been there the last time I had come in. A silver-haired couple in nearly matching plaid shirts and blue jeans bustled inside, arguing about an interview with a senator they'd been listening to, probably on NPR.

She started loading up on granola bars and grabbed a bottle of aspirin.

Her husband high-tailed it to the back of the store and knocked loudly on the restroom door. "Anyone in there?"

Returning to my question, Dylan answered, "My folks said to speak my mind. Too many people think that nobody in East Hannesburg is hurting for money. Or they think we're somehow lesser than them. You wouldn't believe all the people at school who come in here, and it's like they don't even know me. They never even glance at my face."

Had I said hello to him that rainy summer day with Peter Ney?

Not really. I hadn't noticed Dylan much at first, and then I'd resented him for mentioning Cam, for asking if I was dating Peter. But Dylan didn't have much of a filter. He pushed, maybe because he survived by pushing.

Dylan's gaze was fixed on the video from the store camera. His hand was on his phone.

I took a sip of orange drink. "What's wrong?"

Then the owner of the Beetle convertible strode in with a drooling pug peeking out of her tote bag, the restroom door opened, and Dylan breathed, "It's okay. We're okay."

The guy in camo print left the store without buying anything or turning his face our way, and the widely smiling middle-aged woman with the dog said, "Hello there! My GPS is on the fritz. How do we get to Oma Dottie's B&B?"

While Dylan rang up her bottled water, I gave the lady directions to the bed-and-breakfast. After they'd left, I asked Dylan, "What was all that about?"

"Can't be too careful," he said. "This place has been robbed twice in the past six months."

Landing a Role

Callbacks for the musical were scheduled for Tuesday after the final bell. Adjusting the front seat of Mama's compact car, I said, "Remember, Mrs. Q isn't going to be all about the strongest actor or singer. The key is showing her that you're the best fit for the part."

There was every reason to be optimistic. Hughie knew his monologue, his singing was solid, and his dancing was coming along. The Tin Man was supposed to move stiffly anyway.

"I'm ready," Hughie said, staring out his open passenger-side window at a neighbor woman power walking with two energetic brown terriers.

Unless he froze up, I figured Hughie was a shoo-in for the understudy, which would've been fantastic. Especially for a freshman. But I was hoping for more.

I believed in him, and, to be honest, I wanted him to beat out the jackass who'd made the ignorant totem-pole comment. "Listen to the instructions. Project a can-do attitude."

"Can do," my brother echoed.

As we passed one new house after another, regulation basketball hoops rose from concrete driveways framed by freshly manicured deep-green lawns. A yard sign proclaimed the two-story on the corner home to a varsity gymnast. But sports aren't the only path to stardom.

"Don't forget your towel and water," I reminded my brother. "Say thank you when you're done with your audition."

Biting his thumbnail, Hughie said, "Mvto, Sissy."

"You're welcome." Had I made him nervous?

Maybe I should've kept my mouth shut.

Hughie hadn't called me Sissy since kindergarten.

"Why not?" Daniel asked later at the *Hive* editors' new makeshift command center.

"Unless we go to state, sports go on the Sports page," Karishma said, with a wave of her hand. "News goes on the front page."

Daniel clicked his pen. "It's called the *front* page, not the *News* page."

Erasing the whiteboard, Ms. Wilson didn't so much as glance their way. She'd reserved final approval before the paper went live and handled all the teacher stuff. Otherwise, she wanted us to act like we were working for a real-world media outlet.

She had a twofold policy:

1. Don't bother me unless you're on fire.
2. Don't catch on fire.

Joey had been excused to do a follow-up interview for his senior-photos story. Nick was copyediting Emily's piece on Marching Band while Alexis called an ACT prep instructor for a quote. The day before, Alexis had successfully pitched her editorial: encouraging students to foster baby animals from the local shelter until they were old enough to adopt.

Nick had filled me in on my fellow girl reporters after French class.

Emily knew everybody. Everybody knew her and she didn't give a damn what they thought. She wore flowing full-length skirts and dresses and canvas sandals to show off her toe rings, and she was a total potty mouth. Emily had a lot of older brothers and a lot of attitude.

Alexis, on the other hand, didn't seem to know anybody and nobody knew her, either. She cared too much what people thought and had joined the *Hive* to push past her shyness. Alexis usually wore her shoulder-length blond hair in a ponytail and spent quality time at the new skate park. Other than her younger sister, Alexis was the only known student at EHHS who was a member of the Church of Jesus Christ of Latter-day Saints.

I hit Send on my questions for a junior doing a semester at sea and wandered over to our bickering leaders. Daniel was saying, "I'm not talking about all

Cam Ryan, all the time. One of our girl gymnasts and one of our boy runners are returning champs. Another girl on the gymnastics team came in third last year at state. They're big news *throughout* the season."

"Let me think about it," Karishma said. "Lou, did you have something?"

Having botched my last attempt at the feature I was about to propose, I'd done more prep this time. Studied materials from the school counselor and stopped by the library, too. "I'd like to reboot and expand my bullying idea into a series of articles. I can do new interviews for an article about verbal bullying. I could also tackle social, physical, cyber, sexual, and prejudicial bullying. Not necessarily in that order."

Karishma's standards were exacting. I had to be careful about how I framed my goals.

Frowning, I admitted, "It's tough, getting students to go on the record. Whichever subtopic comes together, that's what I'd go with next."

The editors' work space was covered in local newspapers—the *Lawrence Journal-World,* the *Topeka Capital-Journal,* the *Kansas City Star,* the *Hannesburg Weekly Examiner,* and the *East Hannesburg Gazette.*

They made a habit out of scouring for nuggets that could be localized to EHHS, but Ms. Wilson had urged all of us to check at least three news media sources a day—local, national, and international. And so I did. I also kept up with my official tribal newspaper and listened to *Native America Calling.*

"That would be another big assignment," Karishma

said. "You've already got a series on working students in progress, and we can't limit our Features coverage to a few special projects."

She pointed to the *Gazette*'s lead story on proposed city park improvements. "Nothing to stop the presses over, but this would impact daily lives. School journalism is like community journalism. You can't ignore bread-and-butter stories strictly in favor of the splashier stuff."

"I know," I said, taking a seat. "I'm thinking the bullying series would stretch over the course of the school year, not just this semester. So I'll have plenty of time for other topics. Besides, we have two Features reporters."

"Except Joey is also doing photography and videography," Karishma pointed out.

"Joey insisted that he could handle the workload," I reminded her. "And so can I."

"Hang on," Daniel put in. "Did you say 'sexual' bullying? You're going to talk about sex in the East Hannesburg school newspaper?" In a sarcastic voice, he added, "This isn't Lawrence, people. We're bursting with family values."

Karishma kicked him under the table. "I hate to admit it, but Daniel has a point. The Powers That Be are uptight about anything sex-related. We want to be responsible, not sensational." She frowned. "What're your thoughts on an angle, Lou?"

"For the lead? People labeling girls as sluts whether they've done anything or not. The idea that either way, that kind of talk is bad. No matter whether a girl's a virgin or she's had . . ."

At the word *virgin*, Ms. Wilson had adjusted her hot-pink cat's-eye glasses, but Karishma had everything under control. Our editor in chief had already proclaimed her intention that the *Hive* sweep the high-school journalism awards in May.

It was action item number three of her senior-year plan.

I took a breath. "I'm still zeroing in on my focus."

"Feeling antsy, Lou?" Emily asked the next day. She'd brought in a bouquet of orange Gerbera daisies that had done wonders to brighten up the newsroom. (Her family owned a floral shop.) "Got a hot date? You've checked the time every few minutes since class began."

I'd been trying to write a lead for my semester-at-sea story. "I can't concentrate. My little brother's up for the Tin Man in the musical."

I didn't have to tell Emily the final cast list would be posted after school. Arts/Entertainment is her beat.

"Hughie Wolfe's your brother? He's adorkable!"

She narrowed her eyes. "Bet you anything Qualey posts the list before the bell, ducks out early, and lets the tears fall where they may." Emily looped her purse strap over her head. "I'm about to wander over. Want to come with?"

"You're planning to do a story on slut shaming?" Emily asked as we bounded up the otherwise empty stairwell.

"Sexual bullying," I replied. "So, yeah."

87

"Is it because of what Cam Ryan's been saying about you?"

I didn't want to know. On the landing, I asked anyway. "What has he been saying?"

"Uh, that he dumped you because you're . . . well, he said a lot of things. About your supposedly bitching at him all the time and trying to change him and dictating every word out of his mouth. But the biggie is that you're a crazy nympho, freaky sick. Into kinky shit like leather and whips and whipped cream."

Asshole! So petty, so obvious. So Cam.

Up until that moment, I'd been oblivious. It's not like he and I ran in the same circles anymore. He'd blocked me on social media, and I hadn't been living online as much as I used to. (My parents had always strictly limited my screen time anyway.) I kept in touch with my cousins by text, and Shelby was my only close friend at East Hannesburg High.

Emily said, "Don't stress. Nobody's buying it. Not even his precious bros. They just let Cam talk. Everyone thinks you're a total priss." Which of course wasn't any better.

She added, "Besides, let's face it. Cam might normally be a grade-A bullshitter, but he really didn't think that one through. It's no stretch to believe he'd dump a girl for being a hardcore virgin, but not for being a hardcore sex addict."

This was a topic of discussion?

What the hell was wrong with people?

"Screw you," I said. "I'm a lady."

"Screw me, huh? That's a fucking ladylike thing to say."

Emily briefly detoured to the water fountain for a drink. Wiping her mouth, she added, "I wasn't talking about myself or anyone with a spine and a clue. I meant the ultra-coiffed aristocracy."

As we crossed the bridge, Emily swung a friendly arm around my shoulders and I caught the floral scent of her shampoo. She said, "I like you, Lady Lou. You're an onion."

I bit back my reply. I was mad at Cam, not Emily.

Steps from the auditorium, Mrs. Q bustled toward us, a piece of bright-yellow card stock in her hand. "That's it," I whispered. "The cast list."

Please, I prayed. *For Hughie, please.*

"Girls!" she called. "What are you doing here? Why aren't you in class?"

"You know why we're here," Emily replied, monotone. "I'm covering the musical for the *Hive*. This isn't Broadway. You need all the publicity you can get."

"You're intruding." Mrs. Q clutched the list to her chest. "Move along. Come back after school and find out with everyone else."

Emily hesitated a beat too long, so I said, "Uh, I need to use the restroom."

Without a word, she followed me around the corner, then down and across the hall to the girls' locker room. "Controlling beeotch," Emily muttered. "Stupid, stubborn, fucking beeotch."

Ducking into an orange stall, I said, "That sounded

89

weirdly personal. Especially since . . . do you normally talk to teachers that way?"

"Qualey believes Shakespeare could do no wrong," Emily replied. "I disagreed and she nearly failed me for sophomore English. She's been 'no comment' this, 'no comment' that on the casting controversy. Either she's worried about saying the wrong thing or she just hates me."

"I don't think it's you," I called. It was disappointing that the same faculty director who'd decided to change the face of student theater seemed so locked down in other ways.

As I was washing my hands, Emily stowed her lip balm, smoothed her long tie-dyed dress, and said, "My friend Becs might let you interview her for your slut-shaming story—face-to-face, not on camera, if you promise not to make her look bad."

She stared me in the eye. "You wouldn't do that, would you, Lady Lou?"

"No way," I said. "You can trust me."

The final bell rang. Emily and I rushed out of the locker room, navigating the student swarm, jostling to look. Chelsea's name was up top. The lead. Dorothy.

She was beaming, accepting hugs and congratulations.

I scanned down the list. I knew moments before my brother did.

Tin Man: Hughie Wolfe

Match

The editors had already called over Alexis and then Emily to discuss their respective journalistic learning curves. Alexis was back to work, helping Nick brainstorm his latest editorial cartoon. (His topic of the week? The administration had begun trying to micromanage his playlists for the campus radio station, and he wasn't happy about it.) Ms. Wilson had stepped out into the hall to take a phone call. It sounded like she was talking to her credit-card company.

Joey and I were waiting on deck. "Don't be nervous," he said, checking messages on his phone. "They're only trying to help you achieve your full potential as a *Hive* reporter."

We were leaning, side by side, against the bookshelves under the bulletin board. Both of us with our arms and ankles crossed. We were almost touching. Almost.

I was trying not to eavesdrop on Emily's conversation with Karishma and Daniel, but it was obviously going well. All three had just laughed.

"I'm not nervous," I replied with more confidence than I felt.

Truth was, I'd been an all-star student all my life. Karishma's putting the kibosh on my first attempt at a feature had been an unexpected failure.

Sure, a couple of my bylines had passed muster since. I enjoyed crafting leads. I was more comfortable with interviews, and I'd successfully proposed a more comprehensive approach to reporting on bullying. But would I be able to pull it off?

"Look," Joey added. "Karishma says she'll ease up on the reporters once you've all got more experience. In no time, Lou, she'll just pull you aside privately when you need direction."

Maybe Shelby had been right that he was just posturing, but I'd had enough. "Do you have to be so damn condescending?"

"Lou, Joey!" Karishma called as Emily stood to leave the editors' station. "You're up."

I hated that because we were both assigned to Features, the editors were going to give Joey and me feedback together. Sometimes Karishma took her team philosophy too far.

For the occasion, she and Daniel had cleared their work space, neatly stacking their local papers to one side. Joey and I took seats across from them. I opened my notepad. My plan was to keep my head down, record everything I was told, and then stick to questions.

I wouldn't get any better at the job if I let my ego get in the way.

Meanwhile, I didn't mind listening to their "all hail Joey" duet. He deserved the praise, but I dreaded his know-it-all presence once they began peppering me with helpful tips.

"We'd like to focus on the respective features you turned in for Friday," Karishma said.

Joey had put together a feel-good story about a junior who'd biked the long way across Kansas over eight days last summer to raise money to fight muscular dystrophy. It would go live tomorrow morning. Daniel tapped Play, and we all watched the video again.

"Not bad, huh?" Joey nudged. "I found that royalty-free music—"

"It's okay," Daniel said. "It doesn't suck or anything."

"We're not going to make you redo it to run next week instead," Karishma added. "You get the basic facts out, but the emotional connection could be stronger."

She tapped Pause. "You're coasting on bells and whistles."

The editor in chief pulled up my personality profile on Dylan. "This is a smaller story, an everyday kid story."

I braced myself, but Karishma surprised me. "Lou, you got him to open up. Reading this, I have a strong sense of what it feels like to be a teenager working at a gas station."

Glancing at Joey, she said, "I'm intrinsically impressed by anyone who can bike across the state, especially for a good cause. But I didn't *gain* anything from watching your video."

"Gain anything?" Joey echoed.

Daniel, who wasn't exactly Mr. Sensitivity, explained, "It was a blah effort." Gesturing to Joey's images alongside my text, the managing editor added, "But your photos are solid."

"Yes," Karishma agreed. "They're terrific."

I would've added my praise, but I suspected Joey didn't want to hear from me right then.

DIVERSE CAST TO JOURNEY TO OZ

by Emily Bennett, *Hive* Arts/Entertainment reporter
Updated 1:23 p.m. CT Friday, September 18

"I almost didn't audition," senior Chelsea Weber said. Yet the cast list posted on Sept. 16 named her to play the role of Dorothy in the EHHS production of *The Wizard of Oz*. Performances are scheduled daily from Nov. 20 to Nov. 22 in the auditorium.

Weber explained that, in prior years, she had been passed over for significant roles in *My Fair Lady*, *Hello, Dolly!*, and *Oklahoma!* She added, "It's not like anybody ever said, 'Hey, you're Black, so forget it.' But when people start talking about their 'vision' and whether you're a 'fit for the part,' it's not hard to figure out what they really mean."

Faculty director Lisa Qualey announced in an e-mail to students on Aug. 1 that "every student who auditions will receive fair and equal consideration." She declined further comment.

Qualey's approach has generated some controversy.

"Everybody knows 'fair and equal' is code for lowering standards to give an unfair advantage to minorities," said Rochelle Ney, founder of Parents Against

Revisionist Theater (PART). "It's trying to fix old discrimination with new discrimination instead of moving forward. It's a sad state of affairs when we're so politically correct that the truly talented kids are pushed aside so that some teacher can advance her personal agenda. We simply cannot allow this sort of reverse racism to take root in East Hannesburg schools."

Other major roles went to junior Brent Baker (Lion), sophomore Madison Cohen (Glinda), senior Jessica Davis (Aunt Em), senior Garrett Ferguson (Wizard), senior Taylor Nelson (Wicked Witch), junior A.J. Rodríguez (Scarecrow), and freshman Hughie Wolfe (Tin Man).

All-American Diner

Hughie, our rising stage star, chose the restaurant. After morning services at a Methodist church, we ended up in Lawrence for fancy burgers. Billie's Down-Home Diner has the look of a 1950s joint, complete with a soda fountain, except for the flat-screens on the walls.

My cousin Fynn asked, "What's the rehearsal schedule?"

Through a mouthful of sweet potato fries, Hughie answered, "Every day after school."

"Chew, swallow, speak," Mama reminded him. "Three-part plan."

"He's just excited." Daddy cooed at Fynn's toddler. "We're all excited, aren't we?"

Aiyana beamed up at him. Shiny brown eyes. Chubby, smiling cheeks. Dimples!

Hughie raised a finger, chewed, raised a second finger, swallowed, raised a third, spoke. "Until seven p.m. Oh, except Fridays. Every day after school except Fridays."

"How about you, kiddo?" Fynn began. "Any chance you could spare an hour or so to proof web copy for me? I'm hoping to launch the new Arts and Crafts Co-op site next week."

My summer internship with him had officially ended when school started, but I'd offered to do extra work for extra cash. My cousin insisted on paying me minimum wage, plus ice cream.

"No problem," I said. "I've got time." Or I'd make time.

Carrying his joyfully clapping daughter, Fynn excused himself to pick out a song on the flashing jukebox. His wife, Natalie, was off cohosting a baby shower in Topeka.

I happened to glance up at the nearest muted flat-screen TV. The news ticker reported that a bombing in Egypt had been linked to a terrorist group.

I counted four screens in my line of vision.

Bombing, bombing, bombing, bombing.

I felt the tinge of sadness, the shudder of horror.

Watching made me feel helpless, but it seemed selfish to look away.

From the jukebox, Elvis wailed "Heartbreak Hotel."

Chitchat had turned to the lulling monotone of the reverend's sermon. Daddy said, "I'm sure he's a fine, godly man, but it was a blessed miracle that I managed to stay awake."

We'd been switching off between the Baptists and Methodists, focusing on well-established, community churches. Inclusive congregations.

Compatibility mattered more than denomination.

Only Mama seemed to notice my distress. She gestured for our server to come over. "Excuse me," Mama began. "Could you please change the channel?"

"Yes, ma'am." Like the rest of the waitstaff, Phoebe (according to her name tag) sported a checked pink-and-white shirt with black slacks. She skipped to the service station, switched from the news channel to a fashion channel, and skipped back.

"Better?" she asked. "Once the KC Chiefs pregame begins, we'll put that on."

"Thank you," Mama said, glancing at her watch. "We're ready to order dessert."

On screen, a statuesque model pivoted in a silvery mesh evening gown involving large metal buckles and a baffling array of straps.

It kind of looked like something you'd use to catch lobsters.

Rain touched her beaded smudge necklace. "Can you imagine wearing that in public?"

"I can't even imagine how I'd get into it," I replied. "Or out of it."

"Lawn shears?" Fynn mused out loud.

Aiyana tossed an onion ring into the air and burst into giggles.

Before long, everybody was pitching in their opinions on the various high-fashion designs, the show's lighting, and the celebrities with front-row seating.

Suddenly, on four screens, a white girl with jutting collarbones strutted onto the runway in a shimmery, sleeveless turquoise mini, clear platform shoes, and an enormous Plains-Indian-inspired headdress decked out in glittery white-and-blue feathers.

Headdress, headdress, headdress, headdress.

Our conversation faltered. Our laughter faded.

We turned our attention back to Aiyana, to each other, where it belonged.

Our jovial mood rebounded. When Phoebe returned with pecan pie à la mode, Mama said thank you and asked her to turn off all the TVs.

This Land Is Ours

After school on Monday, I grabbed the mail at the end of the driveway on my way in. Daddy was still at work. Hughie was at his first day of rehearsals, Mama at class in Lawrence. Flipping through the stack, I tossed the ads into recycling, the bills onto the kitchen table.

Then I hit the unmarked white business envelope. At first I figured it was a notice from the homeowners' association.

I pulled the letter out. It was short and to the point.

"There is no place like home."
Go back to where you came from.

I dropped it to the countertop and backed away, reaching for my phone to text Mama.

Later, my parents called a family meeting in the great room.

Mama had already asked me to slip the piece of paper into a large Ziploc bag to preserve any finger-prints. She planned to take it to the police station the following morning.

"Obviously, this is someone local," Daddy said. "Someone who could slip it into our mailbox." He'd already talked to a few neighbors, and so far, nobody seemed to have seen anything.

Beside me on the cowhide couch, Hughie asked, "What do they mean by 'where you came from'? Cedar Park?" My brother's complexion is darker than mine, his hair almost black. He takes more after Mama that way.

"Not Texas," she replied, rubbing her eyes. "Not Oklahoma, either."

My parents sometimes joke that, teaching high school, Mama has personally seen more conflict than Daddy did as a dentist in Iraq. Neither of them scares easily.

Their calm might've been a bit forced, but this was nothing more than an anonymous typed message. Hostile, yes, but they were determined not to overreact.

"They think we're immigrants," I clarified, still stunned. It's not the first time that's happened. Especially in Texas, people would sometimes assume we're Latinos.

No big deal. And, hey, a *lot* of Mexican Americans are Indigenous, too.

But the vile note we'd received that day was no good-natured mistake.

It's not like I didn't know things like this happened, but it's different when you've found the envelope in your own mailbox at the end of your own driveway. It's infinitely more personal when your shy kid brother's decision to step into the spotlight is what triggers the hate.

Rebecca is a slender, lovely white girl with delicate features, but you can hardly see them beneath her overgrown flyaway bangs. She does have what you might call a naughty reputation. Even I had heard (from Cam—who else?) that Rebecca had blown a lot of guys.

Boys say stuff like that all the time, though. After a minor squabble, I'd let it go.

Now that Rebecca and I were becoming friends, I regretted that.

After what Cam had said about me, too, I could relate to what she'd been going through.

This *Hive* story on sexual bullying was my way of standing up for both of us.

At the same time, I was concerned about Rebecca.

Going on the record—calling out your bullies—is fierce, and she was projecting "prey."

She walked with her head down, her shoulders hunched. She had a habit of looking over her shoulder and kept a hand over her cross-body bag.

Rebecca lit up around Emily, though. Over the past few days, they'd starting eating with Shelby and me in the school cafeteria. Emily and Rebecca were close in a finish-each-other's-sentences, goofy-inside-jokes, thought-of-as-a-pair kind of way.

They called each other "Becs" and "Em."

"Can I read the story before you post it?" Rebecca asked me Tuesday after school.

Karishma wouldn't love that. "Absolutely," I said.

We'd strolled to a neighborhood park, and the rambunctious second-grader Rebecca regularly babysat ran ahead to the red plastic slide. Nearby, another little boy pushed an empty swing and two preschool girls affectionately pelted each other with foam lightsabers.

A couple of moms in yoga pants looked on, splitting a thermos of what I suspected was wine — they were sort of acting like they were getting away with something.

Rebecca and I kept our distance, side by side on the blue gingham blanket she'd brought. We'd unfurled it onto the soft grass bordering the play area.

"Thanks again for agreeing to talk," I said. The words sounded oddly formal, especially considering that we'd built a Tater Tots pyramid together that day at lunch. "There's no need to stress over every word. It's not like we're going to run a transcript, just a quote or two."

Rebecca hugged her knees. "Sophomore year, this girl in my class — her mother had died a couple of years before. When her dad began dating my mom, she was upset. But she couldn't stop them, so . . ."

If Rebecca didn't want to name names, I wasn't going to press. "She went after you."

I sympathized with the bully's grief, but only up to a point.

Rebecca reached for a stray stick on the ground. "Calling my mom a slut didn't get the girl anywhere but trouble, so she started saying 'like mother, like daughter' at school and some of her friends piled on. One night, they wrote SLUT in shaving cream on my driveway. Bragged about it at school the next day. Another time, someone keyed the word into my locker door."

I kept my gaze on my notebook, jotting down her story.

Rebecca drew lazy circles in the wood chips. "They still gossip about me and call 'Hey, Slutty' when they pass me in the halls. It's been worse, cruder, online."

Now we were talking sexual, verbal, *and* cyber bullying. I'd have to acknowledge in my article where the behaviors blurred.

"I've lost babysitting gigs because of the rumors." Her eyes misted, but she held it together. "You know, nobody wants a slut looking after their kids."

Rebecca tossed the stick aside. "Sometimes guys hit on me because they think it's true."

Over a takeout fried-chicken dinner, Hughie announced to the family that Chelsea and A.J. (his two fellow *Oz* castmates who were actors of color) had received identical anonymous notes in the mailboxes at their houses, too.

"Blank envelope?" I asked. "Hand delivered?"

Solemn, my brother nodded.

Daddy unwrapped the aluminum foil around his buttered corn on the cob. "Try not to worry about it, but keep your eyes open and look out for each other."

Mama added, "I'll give their parents a call later tonight."

• • •

The next day, on my way to French, I heard the word *slut* in the junior hall and pivoted toward it. I approached two girls talking at an open locker and introduced myself. "I'm doing a story on sexual bullying for the *Hive*. Why did you do that? Why did you use that word?"

I knew I sounded confrontational, but enough already. The school's zero-tolerance policy sure as hell wasn't getting us anywhere.

The girl who'd spoken had about four inches on me and a volleyball player's build. "It's a free country," she informed me. "I can say whatever I want."

I tried her companion. "What are your names? What year are you?"

"She's Courtney Young, and I'm Isabella Ramos. Juniors."

Courtney linked arms with Isabella. "We're friends. We're kidding. She calls me a bitch and I call her a slut and—"

"A hot tamale," Isabella said, extracting herself. "You called me that this morning."

"Hilarious, right?" Courtney laughed. "Because she's Spanish . . . or whatever." After an awkward silence, Courtney insisted, "Bella doesn't mind. She thinks it's funny, too."

"Isabella," I said, "you're not laughing."

Walking off, she called, "No, I'm not."

During Journalism, I interviewed Mrs. Evans, the school counselor, in her tiny office with the *Bunnies!* calendar and the white-noise machine.

She complimented me on writing about "such an important subject" and chose her words carefully, speaking mostly from index cards.

Mrs. Evans said sexual bullying was a way to take away someone's power, someone's voice. To make it seem like if somebody attacked you, you'd had it coming. "It can also be racially motivated."

I stopped scribbling and looked up. "You mean sexist *and* racist?"

"Yes, both." She returned to her notes. "I see the stereotypes every time I turn on the TV. Black women, Latina and Asian women, Arab women, they're too often depicted—"

"Indigenous women," I said automatically.

"Uh, yes, I'm sure American Indians were . . ." Mrs. Evans cleared her throat. "I'm sure Native American women were . . ."

She smiled desperately, off-script. "They did call it the *Wild* West, after all."

Her hand flew to her throat. "Don't quote that!"

I couldn't sleep. Hughie couldn't sleep. We'd ended up binge-watching *The Flash* for the umpteenth time while waiting for Mama and Daddy to return from a confab with Chelsea's and A.J.'s parents at the Weber house. They finally got home after eleven o'clock.

"Are we all meeting with the principal?" Hughie asked.

"Can I talk to Karishma and Daniel about doing a story on—?"

"Hold your horses," Daddy called, yanking off his cowboy boots in the foyer.

"There are differences of opinion on that among the parents," Mama said, joining us in the great room. "And among the other kids." She hugged Hughie. "Right now, the consensus is to not give the haters the signal boost or satisfaction." She hugged me, too. "The hope is that, if they don't get a response, they'll lose interest and move on."

"That's it?" my brother replied. "We're just going to take it?"

"The other families have been living in East Hannesburg longer," Daddy explained, walking in. "They have deeper roots and jobs to protect in the community. Both Chelsea and A.J. have much younger siblings who could get caught in the middle if this thing blows up."

Rematch

Joey ran with a story tip from Alexis on injuries at the skate park.

"There's drama in that," Karishma said at our weekly Features meeting. "Conflict."

She scrolled down. "Joey, I like that you framed the lead around calls for more safety regulations for underage skaters. It personalizes the content to our audience."

My profile of the sophomore running a tutoring service didn't fare so well.

Karishma had called it "nice."

Daniel had said, "Cut it in half."

Having been bested the week before, Joey didn't gloat.

Emily stayed put after the bell rang, finishing up her Jazz Band story.

"How's it going with the musical coverage?" I asked.

"I'm maxed out," she muttered. "But isn't everybody?"

"I'd like to help," I replied. "I don't even need a byline—"

"Does this have anything to do with your little brother?" Emily asked. "Wait. Don't answer that. Hang on." She called, "Karishma, Ms. Wilson!"

They stopped on their way out and veered over to join us at the table.

(Alexis and the boys had already left for the day.)

I launched into my request again, adding, "I know there's a conflict-of-interest concern, what with Hughie being in the cast. But I could pitch in on research. Deep background research."

Basically I needed to figure out who'd sent the anonymous messages, and being on assignment for the *Hive* would give me an excuse to ask around. To investigate.

"Media outlets occasionally tackle stories that they or, say, their parent companies are somehow involved in," Ms. Wilson said. "Like last year when the *Weekly Examiner* publisher crashed his car into that church sign during the ice storm. The way to deal with situations like that is to clearly state the relationship—admit to the conflict up front and as clearly as possible."

She always snapped into teacher mode when we needed her.

"I could run an editor's note clarifying your sibling relationship at the end of every article," Karishma offered, setting her backpack on the table. "That's transparent, Lou."

"I am biased, though," I had to admit. "And not only because of my loyalty to Hughie. I mean, Parents Against Revisionist Theater? They're—"

"I'm no fan girl, either," Emily said.

Ms. Wilson pushed up her hot-pink cat's-eye glasses. "Being a journalist doesn't mean you give up your conscience. It means that you don't confuse your opinions with the facts. Facts are key to reporting the news. Opinions are the stuff of editorials."

THE HIVE

OPINION: EHHS THEATER SOARS "OVER THE RAINBOW"

by Karishma Sawkar, *Hive* editor in chief

7:15 a.m. CT Friday, September 25

The EHHS fall musical, *The Wizard of Oz*, will feature a diverse cast, headlined by senior Chelsea Weber, who is Black, in the role of Dorothy. This decision followed an announcement by faculty director Lisa Qualey that "every student actor who auditions for a role will receive fair and equal consideration."

Weber will be the first student of color in the history of the school to perform in a leading role. This show of progress is long overdue. Theater should be welcoming and inclusive of all interested students, and all students deserve a real shot at landing major roles.

When asked why he thought Qualey found it necessary to make her statement, former faculty director Howard Leary said, "How dare you try to besmirch my forty-three-year record of excellence in public education with your hateful insinuations!"

It's true that no previously stated policy explicitly called for favoring white students in casting decisions. However, that bias is evidenced by the fact that all the preceding productions featured almost uniformly white actors.

The few students of color were assigned to small or walk-on roles.

According to the Hannesburg School District, the EHHS student body is almost 80 percent white, 10 percent Latino, 5 percent Black, 5 percent Asian American and less than 1 percent Other. Previous casts in no way reflected those demographics.

Qualey's approach encourages students of color to pursue Theater by offering them the opportunity for full participation. The result will be productions that fully reflect the theatrical potential of the entire student body.

Weighed against the Theater Department's track record, Qualey's statement of inclusivity has been interpreted as a call for change. Reactions have been both positive and negative.

Overall participation in Theater has increased by 20 percent since last year.

Much but not all of that uptick reflects heightened involvement by students of color.

Meanwhile, a newly formed organization, Parents Against Revisionist Theater (PART), is circulating a petition. It calls for a return to "tradition" and a "classic approach to casting."

The words "tradition" and "classic" are smoke screens. PART's membership is dismissing social and artistic progress as "political correctness" and advocating for a return to the previous status quo. Their argument is largely built on the false assumption that Weber and the other cast members of color couldn't have been chosen based on their merit.

PART's bigotry has no place in decisions about students in the performing arts.

"I can't control other people's attitudes or assumptions," Qualey said. "When I stated 'fair and equal,' I meant 'fair and equal.' I cast based on talent, choosing the student actors who proved themselves the best picks for their respective roles."

This fall's production of *The Wizard of Oz* is scheduled from Nov. 20 to Nov. 22 and promises to be wonderful.

It's a giant leap forward along the Yellow Brick Road.

The Resistance

Sunday was Daddy's only day off, so he always tried to make the most of it. He had trimmed the hedges and dug up a narrow row of the grass bordering the walk from our driveway to our front porch. Stepping outside, I offered him a cold bottle of water. "Planting bulbs?"

I imagined tulips and daffodils bursting forth the following spring. Mama had always been the family gardener, but she'd left a couple of hours earlier to study at the KU law library.

"Nope." Daddy knelt, gesturing to his project. "Take a look."

I made myself comfortable on the concrete step, cheerfully bewildered. He was building a series of six-inch-tall mounds, layering rock and soil, circling each with mulch.

Daddy handed me a square cardboard box bearing a postmark and our address. Mysteriously enough, it had originated from a company in Seattle called Frolicking Faeries.

The packaging tape had been key-cut open. I unrolled bubble wrap to retrieve a four-inch-tall forest-green door in a rounded, wood-stained frame, flat at the base. It had tiny metal hinges and a tinier circular knob. I kept looking in the box and found more little doors just like it, except in yellow, blue, red, orange . . . A dozen or so. "You're building hobbit holes!"

Daddy spread his arms, triumphant. "I'm building the Shire. Want to help?"

I did. That afternoon, Hughie had gone on what basically amounted to a scavenger hunt for props with the Theater group. But when Daddy was stationed in Iraq, the two of them had bonded, long-distance, over Tolkien. I suspected Daddy had envisioned the Shire as a father-son project, but Hughie was so busy lately.

"Nothing in the homeowners' association handbook says yards have to be flat," Daddy declared. There was a full-page list of prohibited yard art, he explained, but so long as nobody could identify it as such from the street, the Shire would survive unchallenged. He'd even picked up some scrap sod from the plant nursery to cover the back of the Hobbit holes.

"You're quite the rebel," I told him.

For a while, we worked quietly. It was about 70 degrees, clear skies. A pair of bluebirds supervised us from an overhead branch. A squirrel scampered across the freshly mowed lawn.

I asked, "When you were in high school, how did you decide whether to ask a girl out?"

Daddy positioned one tiny pebble after another around the red door. "I didn't," he replied, puffing himself up. "They asked me."

Amused, I tossed a pebble at him, and with his palm, he batted it over my shoulder.

I told Daddy about Joey, how we'd hit it off. How I'd thought, assumed, *hoped*, he'd ask me out once he knew I was available. So far, nothing.

"Our limo story, the one about the grandfather-grandson team, got over five hundred hits." It was the *Hive*'s second highest-traffic, non-sports video of the semester after Alexis's animal-shelter editorial, and she had footage of three-week-old kittens—an automatic Internet slam dunk. "But Joey's been absorbed in his own stories and preoccupied with the other reporters', too."

Images entice clicks. Joey's—with his eye, experience, and equipment—kicked ass over everybody else's, and the reporters on staff were competitive in a friendly way. Especially since Karishma had started listing the weekly article traffic totals on the newsroom whiteboard.

"During class, he's always off on assignment or busy editing or other people are around."

"Joey strikes me as a fine young man," Daddy said. "Polite. Respectful."

He took a swig of water. "You see this boy five or six days a week. How hard is it to say you like him? What have you got to lose?"

A breeze carried the smoky aroma rising from a nearby outdoor grill. "Well." I chose the little blue door. "If he rejects me, I'll be humiliated and I'll still have to see him all the time."

Daddy patted the curved soil with his hand trowel. "What I wouldn't give for this to be the worst problem you'll ever have. But, Pumpkin, caring about somebody isn't trivial. It can keep you going. I've had days overseas where your mom and you kids . . ."

"Us, too," I said.

The Underground

Ms. Zimmerman, our school librarian, was fifty-something, dyed her graying hair fairy blue and was mostly unsuccessful at hiding her Winnie-the-Pooh tattoos.

Still, I wasn't surprised on Monday morning when she declined my interview request. When it came to PART, the faculty and staff seemed to have an unofficial "no comment" policy, and the administration spoke in gobbledygook.

Then, at lunch, student library aide Brooke Johanson asked me to meet her after school in the basement, beyond the Pep Club storage cage and the empty one farther down from it.

The subterranean hall was dimly lit, heavy on overhead ductwork, and a tad creepy. I waited ten minutes, fifteen. Again, I checked the time on my phone. Twenty-two minutes.

"The librarian sends her regards," Brooke announced, startling me from behind.

I pivoted to face her. As usual, Brooke's sleek blond bob was perfectly curled. Her A-line dress fell a modest two inches past her knees.

Hugging a book, she added, "Ms. Zimmerman says she's sorry she can't talk to you about PART . . . as they're now calling themselves."

"I get it," I said. "She's protecting her job."

Feminine voices wafted our way from the girls' locker room.

"Shush!" Brooke fished a key out of her bra and motioned for me to follow her past the rest of the storage cages and around a darker corner.

She unlocked an unmarked door, opened it, and motioned for me to go in.

Kidding, I asked, "You're not going to kill me, are you?"

When Brooke didn't reply, I entered and tugged a dangling silver chain to turn on the single bare-bulb overhead light. "Let me guess," I added. "This is off the record."

"Of course. The library, the musical. We've got a common enemy."

We were standing, facing each other, in a cramped walk-in closet. About two feet apart, which was all the space available. Floor-to-ceiling industrial shelves stocked with janitorial supplies stood against each wall. Toilet paper, paper towels, hand soap, and various cleansers.

Brooke reached up and yanked the chain and the closet went pitch black. "Here's the truth: They're not just racist assholes. They're racist, homophobic, control-freak assholes who think they have the right to dictate all our lives. I should know. My parents are among them."

"Your parents?" I exclaimed.

"They're proud members of PART. They think I'm monitoring the library to weed out what they'd consider inappropriate material."

I could almost feel Brooke smiling in the dark. "You're like a double agent!"

"I'm not *like* a double agent," Brooke replied. "I *am* a double agent."

Which would make a splendid story for the *Hive,* but it obviously wasn't one she wanted made public. "Is that what you wanted to tell me?"

"No, I brought you here to warn you not to underestimate them and to give you this from Ms. Zimmerman." Fumbling in the darkness, Brooke handed me the book she'd been hugging. "For your brother."

She opened the closet door, letting in a sliver of light. "Before you leave, count to one hundred and twenty." Then Brooke shut me inside and was gone.

Apparently student library aides were not to be trifled with. I was willing to humor her and wait there a couple of minutes. I was not willing to stand by myself in a pitch-black closet in the freaking school basement for one hundred twenty seconds.

I tugged the overhead light back on.

The novel for Hughie was *If I Ever Get Out of Here* by Eric Gansworth of the Onondaga Nation. It was lacking a clear protective jacket cover or any library catalog markings. The price sticker on the back was from an independent bookstore in Lawrence.

There was a handwritten note inside. A friendly one.

> *Hughie,*
> *Here's that novel you asked about.*
>   *Consider it a gift.*
>   *Your Friend,*
>   *The Librarian*

Testing Fate

In Government class, I stole a glimpse at Joey. Lately he'd been off with Daniel during Journalism, interviewing coaches. Between Cross-Country, boys' Football and Soccer, girls' Golf, Gymnastics, Tennis, and Volleyball—let's just say, there were a *lot* of fall coaches.

"Three minutes," Mr. McCloud announced. "Wrap it up, people."

I'd finished the short-answer section and read over my answer to the essay question. Gerrymandering. Sucked most if the other side was doing it. It was an A answer.

My brain had moved on to mentally rehearsing what to say to Joey after class.

Hey, a new bowling-alley restaurant opened at the mall. They're still hiring, and I was thinking about doing a feature on it, especially if any students are employed there. You in?

Breezy. Confident. I'd convey my vision but in such a way that said I was still fluid, open to a truly collaborative approach.

Mr. McCloud took a sip from his Honeybees mascot mug. "One minute."

I skimmed my test sheet. Was it *electorial,* with an *i,* or *electoral,* without?

Didn't matter. He'd mark spelling errors, but he wouldn't deduct for them. Senior grades scarcely counted, if at all, for college admissions. For scholarships on the other hand . . .

My brain repeated: *Hey, a new bowling-alley restaurant opened—electoral!* No *i.*

I made the correction on my test sheet.

"Time's up," Mr. McCloud announced, standing. "Finish your sentence and give it up."

The bell rang, and he began weaving through the rows of desks to collect our exams.

I held mine out, ready to go. Joey was already leaving.

What if he didn't show up in Journalism again? It was already Wednesday.

Tomorrow would be awfully last-minute to make a pitch for the weekend. "Joey!"

He was halfway out the door as the quiz was extracted from my fingertips.

I jumped from my chair, reaching behind for my purse, and collided with Mr. McCloud, sending papers flying.

"Louise!" the teacher exclaimed. "Watch where you're going!"

"Sorry." I knelt to help pick up. "Sorry, sorry, sorry."

Beneath the desk, my hand bumped someone else's. Joey's.

I felt a *zing* where his skin touched mine.

He asked, "Want to check out that new bowling-alley restaurant? Saturday night?"

Kismet! No mention of the *Hive*. A bona fide date invitation.

THE HIVE

LETTERS TO THE EDITOR

7:15 a.m. CT, Friday, October 2

I've seen Chelsea perform onstage in Lawrence and Kansas City. We're incredibly lucky that she's willing to do a high-school production. Prepare to be blown away.
—Marissa Berry, senior

What kind of name is Karishma Sawkar? Is it too much to ask for a Kansan's opinion on casting The Wizard of Oz?
—Casey Green, sophomore

EDITOR'S NOTE: I'm a third-generation Indian American and a second-generation Kansan. I was born at Lawrence Memorial Hospital in Lawrence, Kansas.

Everybody's talking about Chelsea playing Dorothy, but what about the fact that the two brown boys are playing farmhands and nonhuman creatures (the Scarecrow and the Tin Man)?
Why aren't there better roles for them?
—Victor Hernandez, senior

———————

What if we put on The Wiz? They'd yell and scream if it wasn't an all-Black cast (even though there are hardly any Black kids in our school). Why is putting on The Wiz with all Blacks any different from doing The Wizard of Oz with all whites?

—Ashley Jones, junior

———————

The Unlearning Process

I sat next to Nick while he copyedited my latest working-student story, this one about the sophomore who'd made nearly $6,500 in the past two years running an online shop that sold Mod Podge custom comics shoes.

I'd included before and after shots of four-inch heels as well as a couple of photos of the girl cutting up books and arranging the images like puzzle pieces.

"What if we ran a fast-motion video of her doing this?" Nick said. "The whole process, start to finish. We could bring Joey in on it."

"If he has time," I said. "When's the final deadline for the Sports series on coaches?"

"Hang on." Nick went to consult with the editors.

It was Friday, but the *Hive* never rested. We always had next week's issue to plan and prepare. I was the only reporter not out on assignment.

At the front of the room, Ms. Wilson was reading Karishma's latest editorial, which argued that a Contemporary World Politics class should be added to the social studies requirement. "Very persuasive," the teacher said. "Critics will probably argue that any change in the curriculum is going to be a long, frustrating process. How could you more clearly articulate the need for the class, to support the view that it's worth the effort?"

"Frustrating?" Karishma waved her whiteboard pen. "The school counselor, Mrs. Evans, keeps telling me about her yoga class. She says it makes her feel more in touch with my people in the Middle East." She used air quotes: "'On a spiritual level.' *That's* frustrating."

Was India even in the Middle East? Because of interviews, Journalism was the one class where I could leave my phone on. I used the web browser to do a search. No, South Asia.

Ms. Wilson rubbed her temples. "Mrs. Evans is . . . a big personality."

My latest article in the *Hive* had generated only two letters to the editor—one supportive and one from the PTO expressing "profound disappointment" that we'd used profanity (by which they meant the word *slut*) in the student newspaper.

On the upside, the page hits were—by *Hive* standards—astronomical.

Emily had told me after lunch that my story had prompted some friendly girls on Pep to encourage Rebecca to join. (Meanwhile, they'd started walking with her from class to class.)

It had also created a wedge between the Mean Girls and some of their friends.

A couple of the bullies were insisting that *they* were the real victims, that everything they'd said had been in fun, and Rebecca *really was* a slut and was "just wanting attention" and had "blown the whole thing out of proportion." But, as Emily said, "Fuck them."

A Strike

After Joey picked me up for our date, we got the shop-talk out of the way first.

"I know what you're doing," he said on the way to the mall complex, slowing as traffic crawled around a double SUV fender bender.

"You're going for the sensational hook. You got clicks because the subject matter—sexual bullying—is salacious. But it's basically 'she said, she said' gossip."

Salacious? Seated next to him with my legs crossed, I refused to be needled.

"I'm not pitching assignments based on what will beat out your fungible sports lifestyle features. That's just a bonus."

Joey hadn't had a bad week. He'd been officially named photography/videography editor. At the moment, he was trying to see around the traffic backup, clearly irritated by how close (and yet so far) we were from the highway exit for the mall. "You don't like sports."

"I didn't say that. I used to cheer. I was good at it."

Joey threw up his hands at our glacial pace. "*You* cheered?"

Having wrapped his mind around that revelation, he reverted to dismissive. "So, you cheered for sports."

Now I was annoyed. "Cheer *is* a sport."

"If you say so," he replied, raising an eyebrow. "Maybe I should do a fungible sports lifestyle feature on the cheerleaders, then."

Was he trying to make me jealous?

I said, "Yes, you absolutely should."

"This sport is in my blood," Joey said, holding open the door to Super Bowl.

He went on to explain that his mom had been a star on her bowling team at Wichita State and his parents had bowled in a league together for over twenty years.

"And that's your bowling ball?" I asked, eyeing the leather roller bag he'd brought.

"Balls," he replied. Another boy (like Cam, for example) might've made a joke about that. Joey didn't. Instead, he said, "My mom's, on loan from her collection."

He paused to study the display of Kansas City Chiefs memorabilia — the framed posters, portraits, and action shots — mounted behind glass on the walls of the foyer.

A former KC Chiefs player, the one whose son went to our school, owned the place.

Daniel had run a huge personality profile on them the previous week. Turns out the son's game of choice is chess.

As for Super Bowl, the joint is flashy, upscale. I hadn't expected the starburst light fixtures or the mirror ball. Skimming the menu, I was surprised to see truffle fries, a charcuterie platter, shrimp kabobs, and beef tenderloin kabobs. To think I'd been craving a corn dog.

Joey unzipped the leather bag to reveal two glittery pink bowling balls. One of which had been engraved with ANGEL and the other of which had been engraved with BITCH.

With affection, he said, "My mother is a complicated woman."

Joey reached for the BITCH ball, no hesitation, and managed to knock down a pin or two per throw. Meanwhile, I racked up three gutter balls in a row.

"Straighten your wrist," he coached, not that it helped much. Not that we were all that serious about the game.

Between frames, he showed me pics of his hedgehog, Ernest.

"A serious name for a hedgehog," I said, fiddling with my dangly beaded earring.

"He's a serious hedgehog," Joey replied. "Prickly at times."

What with the bowling, the pulsing music, and the

weekend-night crowd, Super Bowl was *loud*. We weren't so much talking as shouting at each other.

Still, we managed to have a conversation. We talked about his big sister, Marianna, who was studying mechanical engineering at K-State, and about Hughie playing the Tin Man in the musical. We talked about camera-itis and ballet. About how Joey loves climbing walls and how I'll never swim in the ocean because *everything* wants to eat you, even seahorses.

"Seahorses won't eat you unless you're already dead and decomposing," Joey reassured me. "They have tiny mouths, which is why they can only take tiny bites and whistle tiny water whistles and give tiny seahorse kisses."

Which was the cutest, most romantic, disgusting thing I'd ever heard, and I thought he might lean over to give me a tiny seahorse kiss right then.

He bent to retie his stinky rented bowling shoe instead.

When I finally managed to knock down two pins, Joey swung me around in a congratulatory hug. Then it was his turn—a spare!

Dueling with gnawed-clean kebab sticks, he admitted to liking his mom's new apartment better than his dad's latest girlfriend.

"I'm new to East Hannesburg, too," I said. "Since last winter. I'm a Texan—Cedar Park, Texas, just outside Austin. But Oklahoma's home."

"A Texan from Oklahoma?" Joey mused as we got up to leave. "Is that legal?"

Had he reached for my hand, or had I reached for his?

I wasn't sure. It seemed so natural, so inevitable.

I tenderly squeezed his fingers between mine. "Not everything is about football."

Once we reached the relatively quieter foyer, I explained, "My grandparents live in Oklahoma. My parents are from there originally."

The KC Chiefs football photos and paraphernalia caught my eye again.

The frenzied fans in redface, screaming at Arrowhead Stadium.

Did Joey notice them?

I didn't think so. His gaze was on me.

By my porch light, we jokingly debated where to display our future bowling trophies.

"The fireplace mantel is traditional," Joey said. "Or behind the bar in the man cave."

"I'll line mine—my enormous championship trophies—around my front yard like pickets on a fence." Glancing down at Daddy's hobbit houses, I added, "So there, homeowners' handbook!"

"'So there,' who now?" Joey asked. As I explained, he crouched on the front walk to study the Shire. "Geektastic." He started talking about how he'd read Tolkien, seen the films.

Magical, right? The stuff of first-date fantasy.

As I knelt beside Joey, he said, "When my parents split up, they tossed or donated truckloads of stuff.

Holiday decorations, books. They threw away their bowling trophies."

No need to rush, I decided. For Joey, romance was still a tender subject.

What he needed right then was a friend. I set aside my first-kiss hopes and went with a comforting, slightly off-balance hug instead.

Musical Reporters

Emily slammed her plastic food tray onto the lunch table. "Damn it!"

"Whoa!" Shelby said, wiping tomato sauce from her cheek. "Watch the splash zone."

"Your dad won't budge, Em?" Rebecca asked, pushing aside her bangs. She didn't use them to hide from her friends like she did from the rest of the world.

"No, he texted me back and said his mind was made up." Emily gathered up her maxiskirt so she could sit on the attached bench. "Damn those fuckers."

Shelby and I traded baffled looks. "Want to fill us in?" I asked.

"I'm off the casting-controversy story," Emily announced.

She speared a ravioli like she had a grudge against it and then dropped her fork. "One of the PART parents stormed into our flower shop yesterday. He practically threatened my dad.

"If I don't slant the coverage their way, their evil coven at Immanuel Baptist—and anyone else under their spell—will take their floral orders somewhere else from now on. We're talking weddings, funerals, holidays, birthdays, anniversaries, homecoming, prom . . ."

The Bennetts' storefront was in the same strip mall as the Harmony Haven nail salon. It was one of the few locally owned businesses in East Hannesburg.

Emily added, "Immanuel's the biggest church in town."

"They're pissed about Karishma's editorial," I realized out loud, suddenly losing my appetite. "But, hey, she told it like it is."

"They're even more pissed that I've been quoting the student actors and the cast's supporters," Emily clarified. "If we showcase any point of view except PART's, we're supposedly oppressing them somehow."

"They're not an evil coven," Shelby said, stealing one of my pear slices. "Or a coven of any kind. They're not witches. They're not cool enough to be witches. They are evil, though."

"Not wicked?" Emily asked.

"Not cool enough to be wicked, either," I insisted.

"Strongly agreed." Rebecca played with her flatbread and hummus. "Imagine if Dorothy and the Wicked Witch fell in love. Somebody should write that script."

"You should write it, Becs," Emily said, obviously cheered by the thought.

I could imagine Rebecca's vision of Oz onstage.

Someday soon, I prayed.

Given the latest PART development, Karishma, Ms. Wilson, Emily, and I had gathered around the editors' station after school. It was a closed-door meeting.

Emily was pacing around us, radiating nervous energy. She'd asked for the privacy and to go off the record because of her dad's involvement.

Daniel was out on assignment with Joey or they would've been invited, too.

"It's not like we have an infinite number of reporters," the editor in chief griped. "After what went down last year, we're barely making do with a skeleton staff as it is."

Karishma was writing my name, Joey's, and Emily's on the whiteboard. Then she underlined them and wrote COI (for "conflict of interest") under Emily's name. "Somebody's got to take point on the musical-casting story," Karishma said. "A consummate professional who can hold their own, toe-to-toe, with PART founder Mrs. Ney herself."

That someone was me. "I'll take it," I said. "I'm—"

"Joey wants it, too," Ms. Wilson explained. "And he has the most experience."

Karishma spoke up before I could. "But not the best temperament. He blew up at Cam Ryan in the locker room last weekend." She sighed. "While on assignment for the *Hive*."

To represent that, she drew an unhappy face.

That was the first I'd heard of the incident. Joey hadn't said a word to me at the bowling alley or in the three days since. "What happened?" I asked.

"Lady Lou, your name may have come up." Emily paused midstep. "We're talking shoving, cussing. A bountiful display of boiling testosterone."

"No bloodshed or suspensions," Karishma added. "Just a stern warning from the coach."

It wasn't hard to envision the locker-room scene. I knew Cam was still talking trash on me. Apparently Joey had decided to talk back. Chivalrous, but I could handle my ex myself.

"PART is infuriating. Lou, when it comes to keeping cool, staying pro, I have more faith in you than I do in Joey." Karishma added a star next to my name.

Glancing over her shoulder at Emily, she added, "If we had a credible source, an adult source, saying that PART is threatening people . . ."

"Sorry." Emily folded her arms. "My dad told me to make the problem go away. Quietly. I know how that sounds. If it were up to me, I'd—"

"I understand," Ms. Wilson assured her. "Everybody here understands." She turned to me. "But are you sure, Louise? These people play dirty."

I thought of the anonymous message that had been left in my family's mailbox.

I was reluctant to do anything that would attract more negative attention to Hughie.

On the other hand, somebody at the *Hive* needed to keep the heat on PART.

"*I* don't understand!" Emily kicked the trash can. "Why do they get to win?"

"They don't," I insisted. "How about we split the difference? I'll take point on the story. With Joey on video. We can *share* the reporting byline."

Mostly because he wasn't there to make his case or defend himself.

"Thank you, Louise." Karishma reached to briefly take Emily's hand. "Why don't you write the personality profile on Chelsea? That way you'll still be teaming with Lou and Joey on the musical coverage; you just won't be handling the PART angle."

With that, the editor in chief circled all three names, clearly satisfied.

"Do all of your list exercises result in a team assignment?" I asked Karishma.

"Call it a management style," she replied.

Mixed Messages

Midweek, Mama drove me to Daddy's office in Olathe so his dentistry partner could confirm that I still have no cavities and that I floss like it's my Olympic sport. In the waiting room, I closed the worn copy of *Teen Lifestyles* and asked, "Want to tell me what's wrong?"

Mama stopped tapping her foot. "I was going to talk to you after your appointment, but there's been another unsigned note. No stamp. Hand delivered to our mailbox. Same exact wording, paper, type size, font." It had been over two weeks since the last one.

"When did it come?" I straightened in my chair. "When were you going to tell—?"

"Only yesterday," Mama assured me, lacing her fingers through mine. "You had to study for this morning's Calc test. Your father and I didn't want to distract you. Your schoolwork is far more important. These people don't get to mess with your education."

The words flitted through my memory:

"There is no place like home."

Go back to where you came from.

I can't say the knowledge wouldn't have blown my concentration. A second note signaled an ongoing effort, a commitment. It made me wonder what might come next.

Mama went on, "Hughie texted A.J. and Chelsea, and then we called their parents. Once again, the Webers and Rodríguezes received identical messages on the same day."

"Louise!" the receptionist called. "Dr. Lee will see you now."

Later, under a vow of secrecy, Mama took us out for double chocolate fudge Coca-Cola cake at Cracker Barrel. It was our annual post-dentistry tradition, a way of taking a break from Daddy's anti-sugar obsession. "Don't worry about your father," she joked as the waiter dropped off our plates. "He never has to know."

"I'm more worried about those freaky notes."

I'd turned the situation over in my mind as the hygienist poked at my gums, scraped at my teeth. It was the not knowing that gnawed at me. Should we expect more of the same or something worse? "What did the cops say?"

Mama waved her fork. "What I expected. They have to prioritize their caseload, and there's not much to it. No property damage, no bodily harm. No specific threat. The backlog and wait time for running fingerprints is substantial. Then there's got to already be a match in the system to get an identification.

"If something more serious happens, the police claim they'll be all over it, but for now, they seemed inclined to dismiss the whole thing as a prank."

I stirred my Diet Coke with my straw. "Did any of the neighbors see anything this time?"

Mama savored a bite. "No, but it could *be* one of the neighbors. No one on our cul-de-sac, but a few people—parents and students—on the surrounding streets have signed the PART petition, and nobody would think twice about seeing them out and about on our block."

That was a distressing thought.

The Emerald Hills subdivision was by no means well established. Upward of 70 percent of the lots had sold, but a couple of blocks away, new houses were still being built.

Nobody had lived there very long. Nobody knew each other very well. My parents didn't hang out at the community clubhouse. Last summer, we were out of town during the neighborhood garage sale, and Hughie and I made it to the pool only a couple of times.

"You're sure we don't want to go public?" I asked.

"No," Mama said. "I'm not sure at all."

No question, the harassment was news, especially now that there had been more than one incident. What's more, coverage of the controversy had become my responsibility.

I felt guilty about keeping the secret from the rest of the *Hive* staff.

Hell, I wasn't even supposed to tell Shelby. But it was by no means all about me.

Resolved, I picked up my fork, indulged in the chocolate.

Afterward, Mama and I drove to Lawrence and visited the Kansas Indian Arts and Crafts Cooperative, "owned and operated by local Native artists and craftspeople."

(Cousin Fynn handles their web design, occasionally with my help.)

The Native law students had decided to shop there for gifts for their Heritage Month guest speakers. Before going back to school, Mama might've done some beadwork herself.

Across the store, she looked at handcrafted baskets, studied the tags that identified the weavers and their respective tribal affiliations. I was flipping through a book about all the white actors—like Rock Hudson, Burt Lancaster, and Audrey Hepburn—who'd played Indians in movies.

A shopper, her coloring close to Mama's, paused at the shelves. "Learning anything?"

At her smug tone, I tensed. The young Native woman wore a burgundy suit, sensible heels. Clearly she didn't see me for who I am.

Mama strode over, placed a protective hand on my shoulder, and glanced at the paperback in my hands. "Ah, whitewashing," she said. "Quintessential Hollywood."

As I said before, quite the diplomat, my mother. Always the educator.

But she couldn't always be there to take up for me.

"Heaven forbid an Indian actor get a job, right?" the other customer agreed.

I looked for some sign of recognition that she'd been in the wrong, some hint of apology.

And . . . nothing.

They had a friendly enough chat while I returned the book to its shelf and slipped away to peruse the jewelry case by the register.

Wrestling

The red Porsche convertible looked out of place in front of Nick's modest ranch-style house in one of East Hannesburg's older residential developments. As Joey parked his beat-up Jeep Wrangler alongside the curb, I said, "You must love covering Sports with Daniel."

Joey turned off the ignition. "It's a sweet ride. But on assignment, I'm the one who does the driving or we take separate cars. There's not room for my equipment in there, and Daniel's father would have a meltdown if my stuff scratched those leather seats."

Nick had invited the *Hive* staff over on Thursday for movie night. In class that week, we'd half-heartedly considered Ms. Wilson's recommendation, *All the President's Men,* before choosing Alexis's suggestion, *Never Been Kissed.* It's a Drew Barrymore rom-com about a *Chicago Sun* reporter who goes undercover in a prom-obsessed high school.

We paused the film halfway through. Karishma and Joey went to the kitchen with Nick for more drinks and snacks. My phone vibrated, and I glanced at the pic of Hughie, Chelsea, and A.J. backstage with their arms around each other. A solidarity selfie.

"Um, Daniel," Alexis began from the love seat, "my brother was home from Ames last weekend, and we ran into the Wrestling coach at Chili's."

She'd wiped out on her skateboard on the way over and was still icing her right shin.

"When I mentioned covering this winter's high-school meets, your name came up and — maybe this is nothing — but he used the word *if,* as in '*if* Daniel goes out for the team.' You're our best wrestler. What gives?"

Daniel set his phone on an end table. "Last week, Coach said that if I don't drop Journalism next semester, I can forget Wrestling."

"Drop Journalism?" I inched forward on the sofa. "Why?"

"His son's construction company is up for the building contract on the Immanuel Baptist expansion," Daniel explained. "We're talking serious money, *millions,* and as far as the pastor's wife is concerned, the *Hive* is 'undermining tradition.'"

I was stunned. The coach was willing to screw over his top wrestler and jeopardize his upcoming season. But it was a ton of money. Life-changing money that would all go to his son.

It was like an insidious game of dominoes. Peter Ney's mom had leaned on the Wrestling coach to lean on

Daniel to punish, maybe even silence, the *Hive* like she had last year.

I wondered what—if anything—Peter knew about it and not only because of his family ties. He's on the Wrestling team.

I moved closer to Daniel and rested my knee on the ottoman. "What're you going to do?"

Alexis stayed put. "Doesn't your family go to Immanuel Baptist?"

"We used to," Daniel said, like there was more to the story. But then he pushed Play as the others returned with soft drinks, potato chips, and onion dip.

In *Never Been Kissed*, suggesting the prom theme ("Meant for Each Other: Famous Couples Throughout History") helps propel Drew Barrymore's character, Josie Geller, to popularity. The dance itself is a costume ball with partygoers decked out as, among other things, Shakespeare's Rosalind and Orlando, the tortoise and the hare, various Barbie dolls, a double helix, Robin Hood and Maid Marian, Sandy and Danny from *Grease*, Joseph with a very pregnant Mary, and, for no apparent reason, Hollywood Indians.

On our way home, Joey tossed me a blanket (it was chilly, what with the October night air and the non-existent Jeep floorboards) and I filled him in on the Daniel situation. I added, "Speaking of sports, rumor has it you exchanged a few words with my ex in the locker room."

I was impressed. Joey had stood up to Cam Ryan's

bullying and didn't seem to give a damn about the social ramifications. But still.

"I knew guys like him at West Overland," Joey said, turning into my subdivision. "I grew up with them, hung out with them, played ball with them."

Two streets farther, on the corner lot, a number 5 made of pink balloons had been centered in the yard. (Somebody had a birthday.) Joey added, "What I don't understand about you and Ryan: What the hell did the two of you ever talk about? The guy's a troglodyte."

It was refreshing, dating a boy with a vocabulary. Big picture, Joey and I did have more in common. We'd both chosen Journalism over the typical paths to popularity. Both of our dads were veterans, and both of us were bicultural. I could joke around with him, embrace my bookish inner dork (and type-triple-A overachiever). "Mostly Cam and I talked about him."

"Figures," Joey said as we cruised beneath a streetlight. "Cam Ryan is the single most narcissistic, self-absorbed—"

"Sometimes," I agreed. *Narcissistic*—that was the word Shelby always used to describe Cam. I didn't want to dredge up the specifics of what had started the fight between the boys.

I'd been trying not to fixate on what my ex had been saying about me.

"But Cam's also of the past," I said. "My past. I don't love him anymore. I'm not dating him anymore. If he can't stop talking about me, I'll be the one to decide whether to ignore him or shut him down."

"You *loved* him?" Joey exclaimed, turning down the heat.

That *would* be the one thing I said that he grabbed onto. Was it about jealousy, or was Joey rightly horrified that someone I'd been in love with could bad-mouth me that way?

"No," I said. "Maybe. I used to think I did."

My house was in sight. Mama had left the porch light on. Between Joey and me, tonight had felt more like a friend thing than a romantic thing. Especially after talking about Cam.

At this rate, I wasn't doing any better with kisses than Drew Barrymore's character.

Deliciously Divine

"Why would someone from Germany bother with Bierfest in Hannesburg, Kansas?" I asked the following weekend over the bouncy Bavarian oompah music.

"Why do American tourists go to McDonald's in Munich?" the exchange student replied.

On Columbus Day—make that Indigenous People's Day—leaves blew crimson and gold. The scent of smoked sausage filled the air. A hearty, white-haired lady handed me a flyer advertising the historical society's walking tour.

Joey and I filmed a quick interview with the EHHS sophomore who was handing out free lemonade and brochures for Oma Dottie's B&B. He typically handled their summer yard work, cleared winter snow and ice, and helped change out the holiday decorations.

Joey had already captured footage of the one-mile fun run, the parade, the horseshoe tournament, and the antique-tractor show.

We'd also talked to more than a few jovial locals who'd already had their fair share of microbrewed beer or hard cider. And it wasn't even noon yet.

Joey fired a series of still shots of Rain, in a dirndl, and Dmitri, in a Harvesters jersey and jeans, coming off the carousel. Football aside, he had a solid Clark Kent quality that she seemed charmed by. Both were sporting all-access wristbands for the carnival rides.

"That's my cousin!" I exclaimed, waving them over.

Joey keyed in their names for the captions. "H-E-A-D-B-I-R-D," he repeated. "Like a compound word. Got it. That's a new one on me."

Dmitri took it in stride. "I've never met a Kairouz before, either."

That reminded me: when Joey and I first met, I'd said almost the same thing.

We found Marie and Queenie playing ringtoss and Hughie in line for fried blueberry pie. The twins showed us photos of the 1970s split-level that their parents had put an offer on. Rain and Joey talked Canon versus Nikon, camera envy, and photo websites.

I texted a few pics of my own to Shelby, who, as usual, was working that day.

When Joey wasn't looking, Rain flashed me a thumbs-up.

• • •

"You and Rain look enough alike to be sisters," Joey said as we neared the top of the Ferris wheel.

I was flattered. My cousin is a total sweetheart and one of those girls who's so exquisite it's like you're shocked to see her in real life. Whereas my best feature, hands down, is my brain. But there is a family resemblance, I suppose.

"Thank you," I said. "Are you close to your cousins in Lebanon?"

Joey did a double take. "Forgot I told you about that. Nah, my family's been here since my great-grandparents." His shoulder bumped mine. "I'm a Kansas kid."

From up high, I could see the water tower, and the elementary school on the hill. All the way to Blue Heaven Trailer Park, where the Headbirds lived, and to Garden of Roses Cemetery, where Rain's mama was buried.

Immediately below us, festivalgoers hoisted beer steins, waved tiny German flags, and swooped and swirled on a ride called the Twister.

At two o'clock, Joey had to leave to visit his dad in Kansas City, so I walked him to his Jeep in the field roped off for overflow festival parking. I hated to see him go, but I had my own plans. That night Hughie and I would be staying over at my cousins' house, and we'd meet up with my parents at our newly selected home church in old town come morning.

I heartily approved of our decision. Cozy congregation. Built-in extended-family time. Besides, outside of Lawrence, First Baptist was one of the few local houses of worship with a rainbow on the welcome banner and a program to help resettle refugees.

As Joey stowed his equipment, I asked, "Do you believe in God?"

He blinked. "That's a big question for a guy digesting three sausage-stuffed pretzels."

"Yeah, well, the nice man at the booth warned you that the third one might be overkill."

"I believe . . ." Joey leaned sideways against the Jeep, rested his hands on my waist. "I believe in kissing you."

My phone pinged, and I shut it off. "I believe in kissing you first."

I savored the salt on his lips. I savored the spices. As oompah music played on, I savored Joey himself for another half hour. It was a mutual affirmation of faith.

Hallelujah.

Hard News

The last time I'd seen Mrs. Ney had been at the Immanuel Baptist potluck the previous spring on the church lawn. Though her son Peter and I had chatted at length, she and I had spoken only long enough to shake hands.

At the time, I hadn't thought about how white the crowd was.

Now I knew better. If you're talking a thirty-five-hundred-person congregation in Douglas County, Mama and Hughie shouldn't have been the only two obviously brown people there.

After a week of ignoring my *Hive* interview requests, Mrs. Ney had insisted on choosing the location. That's why her church was our backdrop.

"Product placement," Joey had mocked on the way over.

We'd arrived early so he could film the main chapel from a distance. Joey muttered, "I'm sure as hell getting that cross and bell tower in the establishment shot."

Microphone in hand, I stood toe-to-toe with PART's spokesperson. She didn't show any sign of remembering me, but in fairness, it's a big church. Visitors come and go.

No matter what I tried, Mrs. Ney stuck to her favorite catchphrases, "reverse racism" and "political correctness."

I wouldn't have been the least bit surprised if she'd sent the nasty, anonymous notes herself. It took all of my self-discipline not to ask.

"What about the student actors?" I pressed instead. "High-school theater is supposed to be about arts education. With that in mind, what's wrong with Chelsea playing Dorothy? Doesn't she deserve the same educational opportunities as everybody else?"

"I certainly have no problem with Chelsea Weber," Mrs. Ney said, dressed in a navy skirt-suit, the jacket buttoned to her collar. "Not that I know her personally, but I am a Christian woman. Jesus has filled my heart with love."

I'm a Christian girl. A Christian young woman, and heaven help me, I almost threw up my bacon-egg breakfast tacos all over her navy kitten heels.

Mrs. Ney held her hands, clutched together, at her waist. "But casting a Black Dorothy Gale is an academic travesty. It makes no sense. The character is supposed to be from Kansas."

So many levels of wrong—how to pick?

I went with the quickest, most obvious choice. "Chelsea is from Kansas."

Mrs. Ney ignored that. "And they've got a Mexican Scarecrow, and what's that other kid, the Tin Man? Are they here legally? We've got to be vigilant. It's a national-security issue."

To keep my brain from exploding, I turned to face the camera. "That's all we have time for today. Thank you, Rochelle Ney of Parents Against Revisionist Theater.

"This is Louise M. Wolfe with Joseph A. Kairouz, reporting for the *Hive,* and viewers should know that freshman Hughie Wolfe, in the role of the Tin Man, is my brother."

The next day, someone slid an unmarked envelope inside my locker. I opened it.

"There is no place like home."

Go back to where you came from.

I glared up and down the hall, scanning faces.

Searching for signs of guilt, but people like that, they don't feel guilty, right?

They think they're on the side of the angels.

They think they're justified.

The Art of the Dodge

"I'm not worried, but a lot of students are worried that it looks suspicious." Tanner Perkins was fair and freckled, with an affection for novelty bow ties. "They're worried that that it might *be* suspicious." It was ten days until Halloween. Today's tie pattern was vampire bats.

Tanner normally would've never deigned to ride the bus to school, but his folks had busted him for smoking weed, taken away his key fob and phone, and told him he had no choice.

"What's suspicious?" I asked. "Who's worried? The Student Council?"

"No, no," he assured me. "There's been no reason for Stu-Co to discuss the cast of the musical. Why would we? I'm talking about people at school in general."

It was midweek. In the back row of the yellow bus, seated right behind him, I'd taken my reporting efforts up a notch. "What do *you* think?"

"Let's consider the facts, shall we?" Tanner's arm was casually draped over the back of the green vinyl bench. "This is East Hannesburg, right? It's a mostly white school. Not an all-white school but a mostly white school. All of a sudden, the new Theater teacher decides to parade minorities across the stage and—boom!—*three* of them land major roles. On their own merit? *Three* of them? A lot of people are asking, what're the odds?"

Tanner clearly loved being interviewed. He'd spelled his name for me twice to make sure I'd get it right. We hit a pothole—hard—and I asked, "Is that a problem? And if so, why?"

"It's what you call 'a possible indicator,'" he replied. "You know what an indicator is?"

After checking to make sure my phone app was recording, I said, "I know what an indicator is. I'm sure *Hive* readers do, too."

"Did you know that soon—I'm not sure when but really soon—America is going to be a minority-majority country? White people are going to be outnumbered. That's scary."

Outside the pristine bus, a blur of subdivisions gave way to a blur of strip malls. Inside the bus, most of the kids were dozing and Tanner had insinuation down to art. "Scary why?"

He straightened his vampire-bat bow tie. "No comment."

• • •

Of the fourteen houses on my cul-de-sac, only three were home to EHHS students. Most of the families had younger kids. The Marino sisters, from the end of the street, went to a Catholic high school in Lawrence. Julia Fuller, who lived catty-corner from us, was a junior.

The Fullers' home design was a mirror image of ours with the exact same neutral paint scheme. The most remarkable thing about them was that they all wore braces on their teeth. Even the parents. (Maybe they got a family discount?)

Julia's were lavender. Her eight-year-old brother Landon's were blue.

After dinner on Thursday, she was running down the middle of the street, teaching Landon to fly his manta-ray-shaped kite. I watched them for a while from my front porch and then wandered over once he seemed to have gotten the hang of it.

A big sister, a little brother. Like Hughie and me.

Leaning against her freestanding mailbox, Julia replied, "Oh, no, my family? We're not like those awful PART people."

She gestured to her kid brother, sailing the manta ray clear of the treetops.

"Last summer, Hughie stuck up for Landon at the neighborhood park when one of the bigger boys wouldn't let him play Frisbee golf. We've already promised to take Landon to the school musical. Hughie's his hero."

It was challenging to hold up my phone to record

and jot notes at the same time. "Your whole family's buy-ing tickets?"

That was good news. According to Emily, early sales had been sluggish.

"Not my dad, he's . . . not an artsy kind of guy. He's more of a sports guy."

We only had a few more moments of sunlight. Two middle-school girls playing basketball in a driveway down the street had just called it quits.

Julia hollered to Landon to reel in the kite.

I said, "Well, sports are ever popular."

"Right, if Hughie was on Football, my dad would be sure to cheer him on. He says that on the field, the only color that matters is Honeybee orange."

She paused. "But can I tell you something? Not for the newspaper. Something personal?"

I understood why people wanted to go off the record so often, but it was frustrating having to leave out the juicy quotes. I tapped Stop on my phone. "What is it?"

"Landon!" Julia called again. "Now!" In a quieter voice, she said, "We were all talking about the musical at dinner one night. I mentioned that Chelsea was going to play Dorothy, and, out of nowhere, my parents both said it was 'fine and dandy' to watch Black people performing onstage or playing sports, but they weren't looking for another Black president anytime soon."

I remembered Mama saying a neighbor could be behind the notes we'd received.

Julia yelled for Landon to hurry. "I've heard them

162

make certain comments, talking to older people in my family, but I never thought . . . I didn't realize."

I wasn't sure what she wanted to hear. It wasn't up to me to forgive her, and it wasn't Julia who was in the wrong. I kept it simple, from one big sis to another.

"You're not your parents," I said.

Horrors

Homecoming weekend came and went, and I barely registered that Cam had been crowned king. Every day, Joey and I texted, talked, touched. My skin melted beneath his kisses.

The party pic of him and his ex-girlfriend vanished from his locker.

By Halloween, we were officially a couple. He came over to my house to help me hand out treats. When I answered the front door, Joey said, "Happy Día de los Muertos!"

I hugged him. "Spanish class?"

"My mother's a Hallmarker," Joey reminded me. "I have a heightened awareness of all things holiday."

More like a Hallmark-level awareness, I thought. Día de los Muertos is a totally different holiday—a major occasion in Texas but not so much in the Kansas suburbs.

He went on, "Speaking of which, I brought what you asked for and left it in the back seat of my Jeep like you said, but—"

"Shhh!" I fiercely whispered. "They're still here."

Mama and Daddy descended the curved staircase dressed as Galadriel and Gandalf.

That night Daddy's dentistry partner was throwing a party in Olathe.

I exclaimed, "You two look magical!"

"Who are you supposed to be?" Joey asked, teasing.

"Who am I supposed to be?" Daddy exclaimed. "Pumpkin, I thought your new boyfriend was perfect. Now I'm not sure we should leave you here alone with him."

"We're leaving." Mama tugged his draping sleeve. "Here we go!"

"I shut the puppies in the master bath with a pee pad," Daddy said as he was dragged out. "Goodies for the trick-or-treaters are on the kitchen island."

"Good-bye!" Mama called. "Have fun, kids!"

The front door closed. They were off. Hughie had already left in an astronaut costume to join his thespian friends. But first he'd given my covert plan his personal blessing.

"The coast is clear!" I grabbed Joey's shirt and pulled him closer. "What'd you bring?"

"Mini Reese's Peanut Butter Cups, Kit Kat bars, and Fun Size Butterfinger bars in a plain brown paper bag, just like you asked. But didn't your dad just say—?"

"Follow me." I let go, led Joey into the kitchen, and

held open the bag of "goodies" Daddy had left. Dental floss, travel-size toothpaste, and sugar-free gum.

"I'm the daughter of a dentist. My whole life, every year on Halloween, we've been the most boring house in the neighborhood." I raised my fist, defying fate. "It ends tonight!"

"Hmm." Joey grabbed two handfuls of Daddy's "treats" and dropped them into the plastic punch bowl on the counter. "We'll have to give away all this, too, or he'll get suspicious."

It was almost sunset. Back in the foyer, Joey made a show of peeking out the window first before running for the candy.

He was so freaking cute. I felt guilty about not telling him about the mean-spirited notes. But I had to adhere to the affected families' wishes, including my parents' wishes.

Joey was like Karishma—he really took journalism to heart. If he knew everything that had been going on, he'd have felt honor-bound to report on it for the *Hive*.

Meanwhile, I started plugging in the lights and audio. Because Outdoor Holiday Decorations was one comprehensive category in the homeowners' association bylaws, the few "Halloween is the devil's playground" residents had to suck it or they'd lose Christmas and Easter, too.

Daddy had gone all out. Translucent spider-shaped LEDs dangled from tree branches. Creaks, moans, screams, and ominous thunder wafted from hidden speakers. Five candlelit jack-o'-lanterns lined the front porch. Scarecrows kicked back in the Adirondack chairs, and construction-paper crows had been taped to our large picture window.

The banner hanging over our front door read BOO!

On the sly, my father had taken advantage of his very public decorating effort to install a security camera without the neighbors noticing. Whenever anyone paused at the mailbox or approached the front door, we'd have a video record of it.

"You don't mind staying in tonight?" I asked, licking peanutty chocolate off my fingertips as Joey and I moved into the great room. We'd tried to order tickets for Dungeon of the Damned in Lawrence, but they were sold out and my parents had vetoed our driving "all that way" to a haunted house in Kansas City on such a hard-partying holiday.

"We don't need to go into the world for scary fun." Joey relaxed into the cowhide sofa. "All the scary fun is already here."

He tossed a mini peanut-butter cup into his mouth. "Speaking of scary, though, have your parents gotten any e-mails about Ms. Wilson?"

I reached for the TV remote to start *The Cabin in the Woods*. "What kind of e-mails?"

"E-mails from PART saying our Journalism teacher is 'contaminating' us with 'bleeding-heart nonsense'?" He explained that his mother had mentioned in passing having received a half dozen of them, all of which she'd deleted.

"They've got nothing on Mom," Joey said. "We just moved here. She's too busy rebuilding her own life to mess with them. But I guess our interview with Mrs. Ney didn't satisfy PART. They still think the *Hive* is biased."

No surprise there. "And they're blaming Ms. Wilson," I concluded.

If anything, she went out of her way not to talk politics in class, even though it was obviously killing her at times not to.

She did have a lot to say about freedom of the press. But that was Amendment One of the U.S. Constitution, and she was a *Journalism* teacher.

"I've been asking around," Joey said. "PART also contacted Nick's parents. Alexis's. As it turns out, they're just fine with 'bleeding-heart nonsense.' Alexis's dad also said he didn't need a bunch of 'loudmouthed busybodies' telling him how to raise his kid. Nothing went out to Emily's folks, though, or Daniel's or Karishma's."

"PART has already tried to shut down Emily and Daniel in other ways," I said, letting Joey pull me onto his lap. "Or at least they're trying with Daniel."

If our managing editor had decided between going out for Wrestling or sticking with the *Hive* next semester, he hadn't mentioned it.

"With her pro-musical editorial, Karishma's their Public Enemy Number One."

"They weren't able to break her last year," Joey reminded me. "If anything, she's come back tougher than ever. I'm guessing it's a hit-or-miss effort. To the extent that they have a coherent strategy, they're probably trying to identify easier targets."

Come to think of it, I did remember Mama replying to an e-mail from Mrs. Ney early in the school year. I said, "I'm pretty sure my parents have been off that mailing list for a while."

"I tried to talk to Ms. Wilson," Joey put in. "But she said to let her worry about it."

He kissed my earlobe, and as if on cue, the doorbell rang. The puppies kicked off their bark-a-thon. Pint-size sugar hunters waited impatiently on the front step.

The most spooktacular night of the year had officially begun.

"Duty calls," Joey said as we rose from the cowhide cushions.

The doorbell rang, again and again, for hours.

"Trick or treat!" sang out miniature superheroes, Jedi, ladybugs, zombies, fairies, vampires, princesses, vampire princesses, pirates, the Statue of Liberty, Waldo, a nurse, a soldier, an angel, a werewolf, two ghosts, three black cats, a Cowardly Lion, and a bunch of grapes (purple balloons, floppy green hat).

Between trick-or-treaters, Joey and I stole deep kisses beneath the crystal-drum chandelier in the foyer. "Next year we'll dress up," he mumbled. "We'll go as bowling champs."

Next year, my mind echoed. During college?

KU was my first choice. K-State was his. It wasn't

impossible that we could stay together, especially if he liked me as much as I liked him.

Mostly moms and a few dads walked their kids to the door or waited for them in the driveway. Some filmed with their phones. Those carrying costumed babies (a pumpkin, a snail, a tiger, a strawberry) showed them off at the door. Maybe a half dozen (Frankenstein and his bride, a 1920s flapper and gangster, a firefighter, and Big Bird) wore costumes themselves.

Sprinting into the foyer with a Butterfinger refill bag, I spotted the new arrivals.

Plastic blue bling set off her fringed dress and braids.

A blue feather on a headband topped his fringed shirt and pants. He carried a pumpkin-shaped plastic bowl by a handle in one hand, a fake spear with a rubber blade in the other.

Three years old? Four?

They hollered, "Trick or treat!"

At the end of the driveway, their Pocahottie mommy chatted up the neighbors.

Meanwhile, another little girl—a kindergartener?—in a Princess Jasmine costume scampered up the front walk with a firefighter and a *Tyrannosaurus rex*.

Suddenly exhausted, I sought rejuvenating refuge in the sweet combination of sugary treats and Joey's kisses. We deserved a holiday, too.

That Man Behind the Curtain

Before school on Monday, I wrapped myself in a Pendleton blanket and climbed onto our sloped wood-shingle roof to drink in the dense red, bronze, canary-yellow, and tangerine—the autumn leaves more varied, vibrant, glorious in the Midwest than in the blink of a Texas autumn.

A playoff game was scheduled for that first full November weekend, and in the driveway next door, the neighbor's minivan was perpetually decked out in spirit signs and orange streamers. You had to admire their enthusiasm. Their kids weren't even in high school yet.

From his open bedroom window, my brother asked, "Want some company?"

The blanket's design is called Shared Spirits. A graduation gift to Daddy when he'd finished dental school. Holding it open in invitation, I asked, "How's it going with the musical?"

I'd told my family about the new anonymous note that had been slipped into my locker, but we had an unspoken agreement not to dwell, not to let PART win its mind game.

Hughie cautiously climbed out to sit with me. "We're going off book this week."

Opening night was less than three weeks away.

"I've been wondering," I began. "Before auditions, do you think Mrs. Q had specific actors in mind for some of the Oz roles?"

Hughie settled in, pulling one side of the blanket around him. "I'd say Dorothy for sure," he replied. "Mrs. Q wanted Chelsea for Dorothy from the start. But I'm not sure race had anything to do with it. Chelsea is, by far, the most talented actor-singer in the school."

That would help push back against the haters, but it wasn't fair. Chelsea shouldn't have *had* to be so undeniably the hands-down best thespian. Just the best for the role of Dorothy.

"Do you think Mama has time to cook?" Hughie asked. "The boosters are supposed to start bringing in dinners to rehearsals."

Mama had tons of reading for school. At home, we'd mostly been living large on Crock-Pot cuisine, microwaved chili from the freezer, and takeout roasted chickens from the grocery store. Daddy ruled over the stove a few days a week—a rotation of tacos, box mac and cheese, tuna-salad sandwiches, SOS (hamburger gravy over torn toast), and mulligan stew.

"Tonight I'll make up a big batch of veggie pasta salad," I said.

(That, scrambled eggs, and Rice-A-Roni are all I can really cook.)

My brother's shoulder rested against mine.

"Vca fvckes," Hughie said. "I love Kansas."

After midnight, I was awakened by my brother's knock on my bedroom door.

Bilbo and Frodo scampered in, tumbling over each other.

"What's wrong?" I asked, pushing up against my tufted headboard.

I clicked on my bedside lamp, and Hughie handed me a clipped stack of paper. Mostly printed web pages, though the top sheet looked like homework.

My gaze fell to the strike-through and the comment that read *Cut*. "Hughie?"

He pulled out my desk chair and sat backward on it, folding his arms and resting his head. "Mrs. Q had asked me to do a short write-up on the musical for the program. Everyone has to take on some production stuff. I thought I got off easy."

I squinted at the crossed-out lines. After the first paragraph, the one about the series of Oz children's books that had started it all, Hughie had written:

L. Frank Baum is remembered as someone who created a magical world with very different characters coming together as friends. But he was like the Wizard. His public image doesn't match the reality of who he was. Baum was a terrible man who hated American Indians and wanted us all killed.

"After rehearsal, Mrs. Q said I was 'off tone, off focus,'" Hughie mumbled. "She said Baum was 'a man of his time,' nobody cares anymore, and I shouldn't have mentioned it."

The puppies jostled his legs, yipped for attention.

"She says the musical is all that matters."

I glanced at my heavy rattan bookcase. Mostly contemporaries, a little mystery, a little urban fantasy, a little romance. My biography of Oglala Lakota Billy Mills, who went to KU and won a 1964 Olympic gold medal in track. My all-time favorites: Y. S. Lee's The Agency series, my Libba Bray novels, and my collection of titles by Choctaw Tim Tingle.

No Baum.

That said, my inner teacher-pleaser understood what Mrs. Q meant when she said "off tone, off focus." The rest of Hughie's text was straightforward, less personal and emotional.

His use of the word *us* jumped out at me. I asked, "Where's this coming from?"

"Baum's editorials," Hughie said, his voice stronger. "Sitting Bull, Wounded Knee." He'd abandoned the chair in favor of the Berber carpet.

Bilbo climbed into his lap. Frodo knocked over the wire trash can under my wicker desk and began digging. "It's all there," Hughie added.

I leafed through his clipped printouts from the web, reading the headlines:

Oz Author Advocated Native American Genocide

Racist on the Yellow Brick Road

Baum Descendants Apologize for Editorials

It was a lot to process. "What editorials?"

"They're there." Hughie was scratching behind Bilbo's ears. "Flip to the back."

I did. This is what L. Frank Baum, as an editor and publisher, wrote for his South Dakota newspaper.

I couldn't bring myself to read the words out loud.

The Aberdeen (SD) Saturday Pioneer, December 20, 1890

Sitting Bull . . . is dead. . . . With his fall the nobility of the Redskin is extinguished, and what few are left are a pack of whining curs who lick the hand that smites them. The Whites, by law of conquest, by justice of civilization, are masters of the American continent, and the best safety of the frontier settlers will be secured by the total annihilation of the few remaining Indians. Why not annihilation? Their glory has fled, their spirit broken, their manhood effaced; better that they die than live the miserable wretches that they are.

The *Aberdeen (SD) Saturday Pioneer*, January 3, 1891 (following the massacre at Wounded Knee, wherein U.S. soldiers brutally murdered upward of three hundred Lakota people—men, women, and children)

Our only safety depends upon the total extirmination [sic] of the Indians. Having wronged them for centuries we had better, in order to protect our civilization, follow it up by one more wrong and wipe these untamed and untamable creatures from the face of the earth.

"It was a long time ago?" Hughie asked, not like that would make what happened less awful, but clearly struggling to wrap his mind around it. My brother averaged Bs in regular History—though he'd never have heard about Wounded Knee at school.

My AP brain in gear, I replied, "Between the U.S. Civil War and World War I."

Hughie's brow puckered, and I tried again.

"About fifty years after the Trail of Tears?"

That didn't seem to help, either.

"Twenty to thirty years before the setting of the first Gal Gadot Wonder Woman movie. Great-Grandpa Lucas wasn't born yet, but his parents were alive."

We talked until dawn. When my brother finally stood to leave my room, I caught a glimpse of his inner superhero.

Interruptions

A hand waved in front of my face. Shelby's. "Hello, Louise. Am I boring you?"

"Sorry, what were you saying?" I asked as we pulled into the Grub Pub parking lot. According to a new road-side sign, a plant nursery would open soon nearby, and this patch of country storefronts and eateries would be that much closer to being fully swallowed by suburbia.

I yawned. It had been a struggle for me, staying awake through the day's classes.

L. Frank Baum's words kept cycling through my mind.

This is Kansas. Odes to Oz are everywhere.

Through them, Baum lives on.

"Nothing." Shelby parked her dad's station wagon, littered with fast-food bags, empty paper cups, and containers. It smelled like stale chewing tobacco. "Nothing but tuition, money, or my lack of it, and the rest of my pathetic life."

As we got out of the car, she added, "I'm sick of worrying. Tell me about the sparkly world of Lou."

Crossing the cracked asphalt, I summed up my conversation with my brother about Baum's editorials. "I've never heard Hughie talk like this," I said. "He's frustrated and—"

"Seriously?" Shelby exclaimed on our way in. "You're upset that your brother is upset about something that somebody wrote about something that happened *over a hundred years ago* in South Dakota?"

She picked up the pace at the SEAT YOURSELF sign. The happy-hour rush had hit early. "That's not even your Indian tribe." She paused. "Is it?"

"No." I imagined that Lakota kids learned about Baum and Wounded Knee the way I learned about Andrew Jackson and the Trail of Tears. From their own community.

But it was all brand-new to Shelby. Not her fault, but there wasn't time to explain.

She had to clock in, and—merde!—I had to study for tomorrow's French quiz.

I somehow doubted that I could make her understand what Hughie and I were feeling. It was what had happened at Wounded Knee, what Baum had done to fuel it and validate it, and that a teacher, Hughie's Theater teacher, had acted like it wasn't important.

Still, Shelby was my best friend. If I couldn't reach her, what hope did Hughie have with Mrs. Q? "Want to come home with me for dinner later?" I asked. "My dad's stirring ground turkey into the mac and cheese." That was his version of cooking fancy. "We'll have to study after, but I'd like to —"

"Can't," Shelby replied. "I'm working until close again, remember?"

Glass Ceiling

Based on informal chatter and a dozen or so *Hive* interviews, my sense was that well over half of the student body either supported Mrs. Q's vision for *The Wizard of Oz* or didn't care one way or the other.

The students of color I'd spoken with tended toward the more enthusiastic, though Monica Suresh said that "maybe it all happened too fast" and Gabriel Ríos-Collins said that "talking about it all the time just stirs up trouble."

I wanted an on-the-record statement from at least one elected student representative.

Having struck out on the school bus with Stu-Co VP Tanner Perkins, I'd asked Alexis if she could help me score a quote from Isaac Olson, who'd beaten out Karishma for the top spot.

"Sorry," Alexis told me in the newsroom later that week. "I tried, but this semester Isaac's been willing to give me one lousy quote on how—gasp—Homecoming is a proud tradition. That's it. I told him I could get his message out to the student body, but he said, 'Why bother? I'm already the president. All colleges care about is that you run and win.'"

I tapped my pen. "What about Erin Gray, the Stu-Co secretary?"

Alexis flipped through her notes. "Isaac and Erin were a couple last year, right up until their ticket won the election. Then he dumped her for Mackenzie Quisenberry after Mackenzie made Varsity Cheer. And after Erin had done most of the grunt work for the campaign."

"Erin is better off," I concluded as, across the room, Nick and the editors debated a handful of technology-related updates to the *Hive*'s in-house style guide.

"That's not all," Alexis replied. "From what I understand, she'd been promised the VP slot when she signed on, but then Isaac and Tanner *told* her that they'd rearranged the slate after the first round of posters had been printed."

Over the past couple of months, Alexis had grown into a journalistic force to be reckoned with. She really knew her beat. I leaned back in my chair. "You don't say . . ."

"I do say," Alexis confirmed. "I also say that Erin has a free period right now and likes to hide out, do her homework, and listen to music in the courtyard."

• • •

I found Erin perched on a wood-plank bench with concrete legs. As I moved toward her, from one stepping stone to the next, she looked up like she'd been expecting me.

"Karishma sent you?" Erin asked. "After you talked to Tanner, I figured I'd be next."

She had on reflective royal-blue sunglasses. I couldn't see her eyes.

"I sent myself," I replied, noting that the Stu-Co officers had discussed me or at least the story I was reporting on. At that point, there seemed no reason to ease into it. "Do you have a comment about the casting of the musical? Or anything else about the musical?"

The Stu-Co secretary patted a spot next to her on the bench, inviting me to sit. "During Isaac's official campaign debate with Karishma, he didn't put forth any ideas. He just kept asking people if they really wanted someone like her representing the entire student body."

Meaning someone who was brown or a girl or both.

"I read Karishma's editorials," Erin added. "She would've taken a stand on PART's petition. A stand on behalf of the student government, the entire student body. That would've had more impact than the *Hive* speaking out—no offense."

Our entire editorial board was made up of Karishma and Daniel. "None taken."

As I pulled my notepad from my purse, Erin asked, "Could you hold off on that? I was elected under Isaac and Tanner. I'm in no position to speak for the whole council."

Yet it was the council's job to represent the students, and she was still an officer.

"Hold off until when?" I asked, standing. This was a waste of time, I thought.

"Karishma would've been a real leader," Erin added.

I itched to rip off her sunglasses. "She *is* a real leader. What are you?"

Survival Strategies

I jogged to KC Fitness. I met Mama at the smoothie bar, and we hopped onto side-by-side treadmills facing a row of big-screen TVs, half turned to sports, half to news.

A NFL player had been caught on camera shoving his girlfriend into a wall. A mosque in Ohio was burning to the ground. Neo-Nazis were marching at a college in Florida.

As we walked, Mama told me about the Native Heritage Month panels at KU and nearby Haskell Indian Nations University. She mentioned in passing that, in Con Law that day, her prof had led a discussion of libel and other legal limits on free speech and the press.

(She was still, not so subtly, urging me to consider majoring in journalism—partly because the William Allen White School at Kansas is one of the top programs in the country.)

Finally she said, "Lou, is there something weighing on your mind?"

I'd swear the woman is psychic. I lowered the incline and filled her in on Hughie, L. Frank Baum, and the Theater teacher. "Sounds like Mrs. Q just shut Hughie down."

"I doubt Mrs. Qualey expected such a huge push-back against her casting decisions," Mama mused aloud. "No matter how committed she might feel, it's still been a stressful ordeal. The last thing she probably wants is to hear about *any* other issue with the musical."

"Mrs. Q isn't speaking out," I observed.

"The show is her statement," Mama countered. "It'll speak for her."

I took a drink from my water bottle. "Finding out about Baum changes how Hughie feels about playing the Tin Man."

"Baum was a monster." Mama wiped her neck with a white hand towel. "But, if you break it down, the musical isn't the Oz books, and neither of those are the man himself."

She sounded so matter-of-fact.

A spin class had begun on the other side of the weight machines. I had to raise my voice to be heard over the instructor on the speaker system. "Is that really how you feel about it?"

"That's what I think," Mama replied, lowering the incline. "It's how my lawyer brain breaks down and ana-lyzes conflicts from different angles."

I tightened my grip on the handrails. "But how do you *feel*?"

She exhaled. "I *feel* like there's too much wrong in this world to fix, but I'm determined to fight. I *feel* like shining a spotlight on . . . what certain people try so hard not to see."

Mama had wanted to go public about the malicious notes, I realized. She must've been outvoted. Mama added, "I'm proud of Hughie for trying to do that in his own way, with his write-up for the program for the musical. But this isn't about me."

She tapped Stop on the control panel. "So far as his role as the Tin Man is concerned, Hughie's entitled to his own opinions. His own decisions."

His own heart.

On Veterans Day, Joey and I covered the ceremonial planting of an oak tree in front of our high school. An alumnus, Specialist William "Liam" Fisk, had recently died in Afghanistan. Army National Guard. He'd graduated five years earlier.

"That's the sister," I whispered, nodding toward her. "She's a junior."

The family was leaving. I called to the grieving girl. I asked if there was anything she wanted to say about her brother. She said no.

I'd never been to Joey's apartment before. It was townhouse-style, located at the end of a row with five other units. Living room, powder room, kitchen, and dining nook downstairs. Two bedrooms and a full bath up. A mix of Pottery Barn furniture, punctuated by antique lamps and showcasing Joey's own framed photography. He and his mom still had boxes of books shoved under the floating staircase and stacked in his bedroom.

Joey stowed his camera, backpack, and shoulder bag in the corner.

I studied the hedgehog's habitat. "Hello, Ernest."

"Careful," Joey said. "He's a charmer."

"So's my boyfriend." I urged him to the unmade twin bed, longing for a reprieve from the day's sorrow, and he was inclined to oblige.

We got as sexy as we could with our jeans on. Bare chested, breathing heavy, forehead dotted with sweat, Joey was — so far as I was concerned — pretty damn magnificent.

Aching to see all of him, I dragged my hand down to the top button of his Levi's.

Downstairs, the front door opened. A voice called, "Joey, can you move your Jeep?"

"Oh, shit," he muttered. Then, in reply, he yelled, "Just a minute!"

I pushed up from the bed. "Where's my bra?" I whispered. "Damn it, Joey, where's —?"

"Uh, I don't know," he replied, momentarily disoriented. "How should I know?"

"You're the one who took it off!"

"Relax." Joey cupped the nape of my neck. His kiss was firm, reassuring.

"My mom's been asking to meet you." Pulling on his shirt, he added, "She's been anxious about how I'm adjusting to everything."

The divorce, their move, the new school. Not to mention Joey's own messy breakup.

"You, Louise M. Wolfe, are a polite, churchgoing, straight-A student from a fully intact nuclear family. You're proof that she hasn't failed as a mother and scarred me for life. She and her shrink are your biggest fans."

Joey tore out of there. He thundered down the stairs, calling, "On my way!"

I found my bra under the bed, wiggled into it and my mauve cotton sweater, and made a run for the living room.

Combing my disheveled hair with my fingers, I positioned myself in the most nonchalant manner I could muster on the loveseat. Then I grabbed a Bible from the lower shelf of the glass coffee table and pretended to read.

Overkill. And use of the Bible as camouflage for accidentally foiled almost-sex might constitute a sin I was right there inventing.

I put it back and grabbed a magazine with Oprah on the cover instead.

"You must be the amazing Louise!" Coming through the front door, Joey's mom pronounced me the guest of honor and insisted I stay for delivery egg rolls and Hunan shrimp.

The Old Clicker

It had been a month since I'd found the latest hateful note, the one in my locker. Emily had remained sidelined from the casting-controversy story. Daniel hadn't mentioned Wrestling since movie night at Nick's. I could only hope that PART had run out of tricks.

The *Hive* buzzed on. After school, Joey sent me a rough file of his video interview with Garrett Ferguson, the charismatic redhead who'd been cast as the Wizard.

Once Joey finished editing, it would go live the next day, one week from opening night.

Given the way Garrett had talked to Hughie, I'd decided to pass on the assignment.

Garrett had dressed up, worn a black turtleneck and slacks. It was supposed to be a personality profile, a puff piece, because Mrs. Q had complained to Ms. Wilson that the controversy wasn't more important than the musical itself and our coverage should reflect that.

But then *Garrett* brought it up, and Joey didn't hesitate to dig in.

"I've had a major role in every school performance since sophomore year," Garrett said into the camera. "I'm a senior, and suddenly, some freshman waltzes in and takes my part."

Was he the one behind the hate mail? I wondered.

Garrett had a motive and clearly held a grudge.

"Was it ever *your* part?" Joey's voice countered. "Or did you just audition for it?"

In the background, the crew constructed apple-tree bases out of heavy plywood and galvanized steel pipes. "I'm stuck playing the Wizard," Garrett said. "That's barely a role."

"It's the name of the title character," Joey pointed out.

"Look, I've got a lot of friends in Theater."

(If that fake smile was supposed to win this viewer over, Garrett could think again.)

He added, "The kid's not a terrible singer. All I'm saying is that some freshman shouldn't get whatever he wants just because of how he looks. Like it's not cool to be white anymore."

Garrett didn't stop there. "All these people barging into our country, taking over. We're practically an endangered species."

Barging in? That was *my brother* he was talking about. A tribal member, an Indigenous kid. I couldn't help thinking it's a hell of a time to be Native.

Or, on second thought, it's *still* a hell of a time to be Native.

That night, Mama and Daddy had gone to Pennington's Steakhouse to celebrate their twenty-third wedding anniversary, which had been earlier that week.

Last August, Mama had stored her beading supplies—untouched since she'd started school—on the overhead shelf with the detergent and the fabric-softener sheets.

Then she'd brought home the plastic clothes-folding board from Walmart, and Hughie had declared the two of us Team Laundry.

While I shook out and awkwardly folded warm fitted sheets, he *click-click*-clicked one T-shirt after another into a perfect square and ruminated on the musical.

Ticket sales were still slow.

Hughie said, "We're under a ton of pressure." *Click, click, click.*

I gave up trying to fold and started rolling the sheets instead.

He added, "It's like, with every cast that came before us, the audience would assume the roles went to the best performers." *Click, click, click.*

"We feel like we have to prove ourselves." *Click.*

"We have to give it 101 percent." *Click.*

"Like Chelsea says, 'We can't let the haters win.'" *Click.*

"Everybody's counting on me," he said. "Everybody's—"

Suddenly my brother heaved the folding board into the wall above the washer and dryer. It ricocheted up, smacking the bottom of the shelf, launching the beading supplies.

The impact popped open the top of the plastic box, and colorful beads burst into the air.

They rained down on us, bounced, rolled on the laminate floor, slipped into the folded laundry, between and beneath the bulky machines.

Hundreds? Thousands? *Kajillions?*

Beads everywhere!

The folding board landed—*whack!*—on the tile floor.

Then—*whack*—the box crashed beside it.

Picking a shiny green bead out of my hair, I was shocked.

Hughie had never acted out like that before.

Last time I'd seen him lose his temper, he was a toddler.

"Mama knew," Hughie added. "She knew about Baum and Wounded Knee. All her books. Her Indigenous Studies. Mama knew before I auditioned. She should've told me."

"She was probably trying to protect you," I said. "You were so jazzed about landing the role. You'd made new friends. You—"

"Now what am I supposed to do?" he exclaimed.

I hugged Hughie tight, wishing I had the right words to explain that Mama wasn't the one he was really mad at.

Honor and Obey

Friday the thirteenth. Game day. Before school, I stopped short on the bridge, flanked by hand-painted spirit signs on butcher paper.

The East Hannesburg Honeybees would face off against Joey's old school, West Overland High. The usual cheers read like CliffsNotes on Manifest Destiny: *Beat the Braves! Defeat the Braves! Sting the Braves!*

They'd been up all week.

But since yesterday, something new had been added.

The last poster now featured a caricature, drawn in thick black marker. It depicted a Hollywood Indian in a feathered headdress, his heart impaled by the stinger of the Honeybee mascot. His eyes were Xs. His back was arched, and his arms dangled to either side.

It took me a minute to figure out that the thing at his feet was supposed to be a tomahawk.

Nick. I recognized his artistic style from his editorial cartoons for the *Hive*.

And there he was, in the bridge's glass DJ booth, jamming to hip-hop.

I marched over and knocked on the door. No answer.

I pounded on the see-through wall.

Nick grabbed a marker and a piece of paper. Scrawled on it and held it up: NOT NOW.

The bridge was the main artery of the school. Students were hurrying by the spirit signs without a second glance. I could've ripped down the butcher paper. That was my first impulse, but Pep or Cheer or whoever would just make new posters.

I needed a bigger, more influential power on my side.

As usual, the popular people had claimed the long wooden benches centered between the floor-to-ceiling windows. I stormed up and pointed. "Did you see that?"

"Hello to you, too," my ex-boyfriend, Cam, replied. "What's your drama today, Lou?"

I shifted my weight. "What are you going to do about those signs?"

"Nothing." He rocked back on his heels. "Last week it was *Beat the Lions! Defeat the Lions! Sting the Lions!* Remember? The week before that—"

"There was no cartoon of a honeybee skewering a lion," I replied. "And, more to the point, there are no lions currently enrolled at this school!"

Cam was gaping at me.

I struggled for calm. "Half of those posters have *your* team number on them. You're the freaking *king* around here. They'll listen to you. Say something. Do something. Make it stop."

Hannah O'Sullivan, a petite, popular JV cheerleader, walked up. Placing a steadying hand on Cam's forearm, she said, "West Overland's mascot *is* the Braves. What's the big deal?"

Hannah seemed honestly confused. Less than thrilled that Cam was talking to his ex, but there was more to it than that. I might've been able to reach her. I began, "It's—"

"Hold up." Cam raised his voice. "Hold the fuck up, Lou. Now you want to talk? Fine. Let's talk about something that matters. You broke up with me by *e-mail*. Do you have any idea how cold that is? How bitchy and chickenshit? Besides, nobody fucking uses e-mail!"

Had the great Cam Ryan just publicly admitted that *I'd* been the one to break things off?

"You were nobody when we met," he added. "Nobody. Now you're nobody again."

I knew Cam. He had zero coping mechanisms in response to having been dumped by a girl he genuinely cared about. So he'd spewed a lot of petty, crude, sexist crap. Created his own reality to explain us away. To avoid dealing with his feelings and to protect his rep.

And it had failed. He still hurt. So he'd repositioned himself from victor to victim.

"You pull shit like that, Lou, and you still think of yourself as a good person. Saint Louise. But I say any damn random little thing that pisses you off—me, your boyfriend."

"Ex-boyfriend," Hannah put in.

"The person you're supposed to love," Cam raged on, shrugging off her touch. "All of a sudden, that's it? You decide I'm an asshole and we're over?"

By that point, everyone on the bridge could hear him over the music.

He shouted, "Fuck off, Lou! Fuck you! You're all *sanctimonious* when you're making everything about yourself, but when it comes to other people's feelings, you suck."

Yes, Cam had mouthed off about me. Said terrible things. He was an insensitive, self-absorbed asshole. But he wasn't wrong about everything. My e-mail had been chickenshit.

I should've broken up with him face-to-face.

By the final bell, somebody had ripped down the spirit signs.

I had no idea who.

Joey's mom didn't come home from work until after 5:30 p.m. On days that we didn't have a reporting assignment, his bedroom had become our sanctuary. Never mind his clothes strewn about or that it smelled vaguely like sweaty socks.

I made up for the lost homework time in the newsroom during lunch. I missed eating with Shelby in the cafeteria, but she still had Emily and Rebecca.

I missed Shelby—period.

But she always had to work, and now I had Joey to think about, too.

Besides, I wanted him. It was as much the talking as the touching.

Oh, how I appreciated that Joey talked about more than food, football, and how hot he was. But again, he had his own history with the sport.

There were a series of posed team photos above his desk, going all the way back to fourth grade. He'd no doubt played a game or two against East Hannesburg.

Yes, Joey had played ball at West Overland High School. Worn a maroon jersey that read *Braves*. Took it off and picked up a camera instead, though football still meant enough to him to display the pics.

I could've segued a conversation from his former high-school mascot to my Native identity. I didn't. Twice I opened my mouth with every intention of saying something—and closed it again.

"What I don't get," Joey began, drawing figure eights on my upper arm with his fingertip, "is why did they stick it out for so long?"

We lay together, our legs tangled. He was talking about his parents again.

I'd come to realize that part of the reason Joey had decided not to go out for Football this year was to spite his dad. Either because Joey blamed him for the divorce or because he wasn't around much and never really had been.

I felt bad for Joey. For all of them. But he tended to

swing between brooding about his parents' divorce and about his cheating ex-girlfriend and ex-bestie.

I was tired of doing so much of the emotional heavy lifting.

"I heard my mom tell my uncle on the phone that she and Dad had been over for ages," he added. "Mom said she'd first realized it on this vacation we took to the Grand Canyon. That was the summer between seventh and eighth grade. All those years, our whole life was a lie."

"All those years, you got to live with both of your parents," I said.

I slid my hand down to rest on his hip. "You and your sister, until she left for K-State. Y'all got to see your dad every day. And he got to see the two of you every day, too."

"Every day he wasn't flying," Joey said. He withdrew, folded into himself.

He wasn't touching me anymore.

Home Improvement

The night before, the West Overland High Braves had defeated the East Hannesburg High Honeybees, and—huzzah—comforting Cam Ryan was not my responsibility.

At the top of the outdoor staircase, my cousin Fynn had just finished painting the front door to his newly constructed apartment over the freestanding garage.

"Hey, kiddo!" An old Meat Loaf song—"Home By Now No Matter What"—blasted from his phone. Fynn's sleek, dark hair had been tied back, and he wore a red tank that showed off the Jayhawk tattoo on his shoulder. "If you're looking for Rain—"

"I'm looking for you." From what I'd heard, Fynn was the hometown heartthrob before he got married, and I'd seen for myself that he treated his wife, Natalie, like she was heaven-sent.

"Well, then, by all means." My cousin gestured for me to come inside. "Welcome back to my Domain. Be it ever so humble . . ."

Fynn and Joey reminded me of each other—both independent, enterprising. They even both drove Jeeps, though Fynn's was in much better condition than Joey's.

The above-garage apartment serves as an office for Fynn's web-design and social-media business. I passed through the cozy kitchenette to his studio. An enormous computer monitor dominated the glass-topped, metal-frame desk. A client website was pulled up, the one for the breakout Kickapoo blues band Not Your Wild West Show.

"This way." Fynn led me out the arched window to the roof patio. He offered me a paint roller. "Do you mind? I'm hoping to knock out the last of the trim before the weather gets much colder." As I loaded the sponge with Parsley Green, he asked, "What's on your mind, cuz?"

While we worked, I told him about my breakup with Cam. How Mrs. Ryan had objected to Andrew's engagement and Cam hadn't understood why that offended me. I mentioned that Peter from Immanuel Baptist had implied that all Indians were alcoholics and, as if that wasn't enough, there were Native boys like Tommy Dale, who'd only date white girls.

"I keep *not* talking to Joey about my being Native, which is . . . Why? We're getting serious. Potentially capital L serious."

I'd decided to leave my potentially fast-fading virginity out of it.

"What's wrong with me?" I asked.

If I'd had it to do it over again, I would've shoved my tribal affiliation into the conversation on day one in the newsroom. "It's not like I'm ashamed of who I am. I'm proud to be Native. Muscogee. I'm proud of my family and my Nation and—"

"Understood." Fynn set down his paintbrush. "You don't have to defend yourself to me."

From the roof deck, I couldn't help comparing the historic, small-town neighborhood to my own subdivision. In old town, some of the landscaping is overgrown and the pools are above ground. I could see the occasional tricycle left out on a front porch and the occasional wheelbarrow alongside a vegetable garden. Laundry fluttered from clotheslines.

There was no homeowners' association here.

"When I was your age, it was harder," Fynn said, moving to stand at my side. "It's like I was Indian in Indian Country and white in white America. Not anymore.

"Being quiet can send just as big of a message as speaking your mind."

I wondered if Fynn might elaborate, but instead, he added, "These days, I've got clients to promote, a daughter to raise. All the negativity in the world, I try not to feed it more energy."

I turned to focus on applying an even coat of paint. "I'm chicken."

Or chickenshit, as Cam would say. Not to mention sanctimonious.

"No, you're smart." Fynn had resumed painting, too. "Sensitive. There's no shame in that. They're good qualities. You're used to knowing the right answer, and you do. But this is personal, 'capital L' personal, and the more you care, the more vulnerable you are."

He dipped his brush in the paint can. "You're not being paranoid. A lot of people draw the line at romance. At first Natalie's parents weren't thrilled with me."

Interesting. They were white moneyed Johnson Countians.

They'd doted on him (and the baby) at the wedding.

Once we finished, I helped Fynn wash the brushes and rollers and pack up the supplies. He led me to the freshly painted front door and gave me a reassuring good-bye hug.

"Eventually, Joey will have something to say about the fact that you're Creek," my cousin said. "It's going to happen. You're going to have the conversation. You're not just somebody walking around with a tribal citizenship card in your wallet and that's as far as it goes. You're too close to your family and your community to avoid the topic much longer."

A Is for Apolitical

"No comment," stage manager Sydney Wood said in the hall outside A.P. Government class. "Not on camera, not off camera. Not ever."

"You don't have *any* thoughts on the casting controversy?" Joey asked less than a minute before the bell. Nobody else was paying attention to our conversation.

A Nerf ball sailed overhead. A majorette caught it, one-handed.

"Did you have to interview Garrett, of all people?" Sydney replied as our fellow overachieving classmates poured through Mr. McCloud's doorway.

Joey's video with Garrett, the actor playing the Wizard, had gone live the previous Friday. Today's rehearsal would be the first since.

Sydney added, "Who knows how that'll screw up my life. Actors are temperamental enough. I wish you would stop stirring up trouble. You're a lousy school newspaper, for God's sake. Stop taking yourselves so seriously."

She was one to talk. "We're not stirring up anything," I countered. "We're reporting it."

"How nice for you." Sydney plucked a large gold barrette from her purse. "You can list the *Hive* on your college applications. This is my third year on crew, my first as stage manager. It's not fair that suddenly I'm expected to take a political stance and explain it."

She smoothed her hair back. "The last thing I need is some college admissions director blowing me off because they've pulled up an online misquote of something I supposedly said to the *Hive* that doesn't jibe with their vibe."

Clack. Sydney fastened the barrette at the base of her neck. "I'm bored. Good-bye."

Pivoting on one heel, she left us standing there.

"Did she just say 'jibe with their vibe'?" I echoed. "Was that off the record, too?"

"It was *off*, all right," Joey replied.

Under the Weather

As I shifted the car into Park in front of the high school, Hughie strolled out with A.J., trailed by Chelsea and her best friend, Taylor, who was playing the Wicked Witch.

According to Hughie, it had long been the girls' dream to share a stage, and their synergy was electric. Most of the thespians were 100 percent behind the diverse cast.

When Hughie plopped into the front passenger seat, I said, "We have to stop by the drugstore—Daddy's coming down with a cold. How was rehearsal?"

"Draining." My brother didn't say much more on the way or at the pharmacy as I picked up cough drops, tissues, and congestion meds for Daddy, sports tampons and acne cream for myself.

But Hughie didn't elect to wait in the car, either.

I caught him staring at a rotating display of Oz-themed greeting cards. He extracted one with a photo of the Tin Man from the 1939 movie on the front.

"Want that?" I asked.

"I thought I did." Hughie slipped the card back into the rack.

Heading home, I cranked the volume on a country radio station. We listened to a song about patriotism, a song about longing for home, a song about good love gone bad, and a song about a broken heart. The musical was scheduled for that weekend.

"It's all tangled up in my head," Hughie said. "The show is going to be amazing, but, bottom line, there would be no Tin Man if it weren't for Baum."

He pulled the Kleenex out of the bag and used a tissue to wipe his nose. "I hate playing a character that he created."

Hate isn't a word we use in our house, not often at least.

"I'm worried that my friends will hate me," Hughie added. "Or think I'm a coward."

My brother was trying to tell me something. With four days until the first performance, he had finally decided to quit the musical. I was the first to know.

The Fourth Estate

When I walked into the newsroom on Tuesday and saw that we had a substitute teacher, I didn't think much of it. Students miss school; teachers miss school. It happens. For a fleeting moment, I hoped that Ms. Wilson hadn't caught the nasty bug that was going around.

"Guess what," Joey said, looking up from his phone. "Elijah and his granddad George finally got a green light on their limo road trip to San Diego. They said our video had been a huge factor in convincing his parents. We can do a follow-up story in January."

I beamed, feeling every inch the legit journalist. Our first story together had made a difference. Joey laughed. "They also said that if we ever need a ride, call them."

"Lou!" Alexis waved me over to Nick's desk. "Take a look."

I bent to read what he was copyediting. Good for Erin! The Stu-Co secretary had come through. The council had passed her proposed resolution at yesterday's meeting. They'd decided to officially support Mrs. Q and the *entire* cast and crew of the musical.

"Do you want a double byline?" Alexis asked.

"Is this your story or mine?" Joey said.

"No thanks. It's all yours," I replied. "You did most of the work. Besides, I've got a musical-related story of my own for this Friday."

The choirs were circulating a petition, calling for "full inclusion" in the performing arts. They already had over a hundred more signatures than PART did, and a 40 percent higher ratio of students to parents. Joey and I had done the video interviews that morning.

After the bell rang, the sub said, "Everyone, please take a seat."

She clapped like we were in elementary school. "I have an important announcement."

Journalism is a working lab. We hadn't all taken seats since the first day, and even then, movement had been fluid. It felt awkward, silly even, sitting in studious rows.

"My name is Mrs. Powell." She pointed to her name on the chalkboard. "As of today, I am the new Journalism teacher at East Hannesburg High."

"What about Ms. Wilson?" Karishma exclaimed, standing.

"Is she all right?" Emily added as Alexis asked, "Did something happen to her?"

"Please take a seat, Miss . . . ?" Mrs. Powell was a slow talker. She kept her hands folded, almost pious, on the top of the desk.

"My name is Karishma Sawkar," our leader spat out. "I'm the editor in chief."

"Pleased to meet you, Miss Sawkar. So far as I know, Ms. Wilson is uninjured and in perfectly fine health. There is no need for you to concern yourself with her."

"No need?" I echoed. Ms. Wilson would never leave us without saying good-bye.

Mrs. Powell forced everyone through the painstaking ritual of introducing ourselves as she checked off attendance. Daniel managed to mumble his name and say that he was the managing editor, but he looked stricken. We all were.

"About Ms. Wilson?" Nick piped up. "Where is she?"

"She's on leave" was the answer. "That's all I know."

"If she's on leave, why did you introduce yourself as the *new* Journalism teacher?" Joey asked. "Why aren't you just subbing until Ms. Wilson gets back?"

"She's on leave." The same words, the same intonation. "That's all I know."

Whatever was going on, Mrs. Powell wasn't the power behind it.

However frustrated, we still had an issue of the *Hive* to put out that week. Karishma urged everyone to get back to work. "It's what Ms. Wilson would want us to do," she said.

I focused on my story about the dueling petitions. A half hour or so later, the room stilled. Mrs. Powell was standing on a chair, tearing down Ms. Wilson's First Amendment poster.

Mrs. Powell crumpled it up, stepped down, and tossed it into the trash.

She replaced it with a poster of the Honeybees mascot that read *Honeybee Pride*.

"Ms. Wilson still hasn't responded to any of my messages," Karishma fretted on the way to our teacher's house. When Daniel had said that he was busy, I'd offered to come with her.

This was Karishma's second year taking Journalism from Ms. Wilson. They'd survived the previous staff's turmoil together. Rebuilt the *Hive* together. And now, disaster.

We found the cottage, with peeling paint, in old Hannesburg on a road with a lot of rental signs. An immense golden brown house cat with a lush mane caught sight of us and sprang from a windowsill.

Ms. Wilson answered our knock, looking ten years younger than she had at school. No makeup. A button-up paisley tunic over black leggings and her hot-pink cat's-eye glasses resting like a headband over her spiral curls.

"Karishma, Louise!" she exclaimed. "What brings you two here?"

"We were worried about you," Karishma said. "The sub said you were on leave."

None of us had accepted Mrs. Powell as our new teacher.

"That's . . . That's so sweet. Thank you." Peering out the door, up and down her residential street, Ms. Wilson quickly added, "But you shouldn't be here. I'm on *disciplinary* leave. Maybe I'm being paranoid, but it might only make things worse."

"Disciplinary for what?" I recalled the e-mails that Joey had mentioned going to parents of a few of the *Hive* staffers. PART had been fishing for something, anything, to use against Ms. Wilson. But I couldn't imagine any of us turning on her. "You didn't do anything wrong."

"Well, there's apparently more than one version of the facts on that." Ms. Wilson's laugh was gentle. "I'm accused of corrupting young minds, I guess."

I ached to write a scathing editorial about the unfairness of it all. But any mention of Ms. Wilson in the school newspaper might backfire and be used against her.

Karishma said, "I'd expected them to come after Mrs. Q."

"They did," Ms. Wilson replied. "But her husband is a semiretired attorney with a lot of spare time on his hands. The Qualeys aren't messing around. They threatened to sue."

The Freaking Niagara Falls of Babbles

The autumn leaves had peaked—amber, mustard, peach, lava, honey, maroon.

I plucked one from my front lawn, held it to the radiant sun. "Burnt orange."

"They don't have fall in Texas?" Joey asked, leaning on a rake.

"For about ten minutes," I said, determined to have one good day, one day that was entirely about romance and joy. "It's summer, it's summer, then ten minutes of fall and—*poof!*—the yellowish-orange leaves drop. The green leaves that never change, well, still don't, and before you know it, it's winter. For another ten minutes."

Opening night of the musical was two days away, Thanksgiving the following week.

Senior year was speeding by. Determined to celebrate the moment, I tossed up the fiery leaf and spun, arms extended. A breeze shook loose a shower of brilliant color.

I laughed, still spinning, while the dachshund puppies cavorted in the piles, digging, forever digging, gleefully foiling our efforts.

When my spin spun out, Joey was aiming his camera at me. He'd been experimenting with slow shutter speeds, motion blur.

I took a dizzy bow. Did I love him? Did he love me?

Would he love the whole me?

I was ready to find out.

We'd stuffed two brown paper bags that came up to my waist. I'd meticulously cleared each leaf and twig from the Shire when Joey asked, "You do realize it will snow eventually?"

"Probably not until after Christmas. At least not enough to stick, let alone blanket the hobbit holes. I'm going to decorate them for Daddy's present. I'll make tiny green wreaths out of miniature pipe cleaners."

"I somehow doubt hobbits celebrate Christmas," Joey replied. "Solstice maybe."

"Yes, solstice." I ached to tell him I was ready, that I wanted to make love.

But did anyone actually say "make love"?

It sounded cheesy, melodramatic, like you thought you were too dainty to say "sex."

Then again, the word *sex* was almost clinical, deficient in romance, passion.

Sex. Meh.

On the other hand, it was a hell of a lot better than "doing it" or "getting laid" or "bow-chicka-bow-wow."

Maybe I could go vague about the sexy fun, use eye contact and body language to say we needed alone time. And not in the apartment he shared with his mother.

Joey and I moved to the porch to watch the pups destroy our lawn-care handiwork. He eased himself into one of the Adirondack chairs. I perched at an angle on his denim-clad thighs.

"So, um, I've been wanting to talk to you about something."

"Are you still pissed at me?" he asked. "Because, like I said, I don't mean to walk away from you. It's only that my legs are longer. We're usually in a hurry and—"

"That's not it," I said. "And I wasn't pissed at you. I was just miffed."

Being Arab American, Joey navigated our screwed-up world from a different slant. But he dealt with bigoted crap, too. I was sure of it.

Hopefully, he'd be able to identify with where I was coming from and shove aside any BS ideas about Native people that he might've picked up along the way.

Only problem? Once I'd established that he wasn't in trouble, Joey took it as a green light to caress my throat with his lips, which made it challenging for me to form words.

Deeply challenging. When I'd rehearsed what I was going to say, I'd always started with declaring my heritage and tribal citizenship, but suddenly that felt too formal and abrupt.

I snap-decided to ease into the subject instead, starting with his own frame of reference. "Um, I was think, thinking about people from the Middle East. About how when you watch the news, it seems like they're always blowing people up or beheading them."

Joey withdrew his kisses, and I took it as a sign that he was listening.

I added, "Or, in the movies, they're always belly dancing or summoning genies or flying on magic carpets or chopping off hands."

He'd gone still.

I forged on, "But my dad served in Iraq. He says—"

"That's enough." Joey lifted me to my feet. "I'm out of here."

I wobbled. "What? No, wait, I'm trying to tell you—"

"I don't need this." Joey climbed out of the chair. "I should've known better than to get all wrapped up in another stupid girl. I've got better things to do, Louise, and in case you forgot, *my* dad is a veteran, too."

"I am not stupid! Never call me that. And I didn't forget! What's wrong with you?"

Yes, I was that self-absorbed.

As I finally realized what had happened, Joey was already getting into his Jeep.

"Wait! You can't possibly think I meant . . . I wasn't fini—"

His car door slammed.

He was gone.

Teachable Moments

Head in my hands, elbows on the table, I stared blankly at my French assignment in my regular booth at the Grub Pub. J'étais malheureuse.

For the past twenty-four hours, Joey had ignored my texts and calls, dodged eye contact during AP Government, skipped Journalism (though, according to Alexis, his gear bag was locked in the cabinet), and taken the elevator with Nick so as not to risk passing me on the stairs.

Joey had one hell of a temper.

I told Shelby all about it on the way to school that morning, over so-called beef burritos in the cafeteria, and again as we walked into the pub.

"You don't even know for sure if it's a breakup or just a fight," she said.

"Yeah, I do," I assured her. "It's over. He hates me."

But the world spun on. A twelve-top retirement party arrived, carrying in a sheet cake that read *Bon Voyage!* An over-sixty ladies' social club claimed the corner behind the foosball table and ordered two bottles of house red. Fried mozzarella was the happy-hour special.

A couple of hours later, a slice of warm pecan pie topped with ice cream appeared between my nose and my screen. "My treat," Shelby announced. "Go ahead — it's medicinal."

I dipped my fork into the melty vanilla goo, closed my eyes as hot-cold-fruity sugar scintillated my taste buds. "Can you take a break and sit with me?"

Shelby glanced around the dining room, checking her tables. "No, I can't take a break and sit with you." Then she sat down across from me. "I work for tips, remember?"

"I can tip you extra," I said — triggering my second interpersonal disaster.

"Here's a thought," Shelby countered. "Why don't *you* ask how *I* am? No, don't strain yourself. I'll tell you. I'm working all the time, like every minute I'm not at school or asleep, and I'm still not making enough money." She swiped my spoon and helped herself to a bite of pie.

"While you're planning for college — no big deal, la-di-da — I'll have to delay for a semester or maybe for a whole year. Or two.

"Meanwhile, you're too busy with your tedious boy dramas and your perfect studenting and your postcard-perfect family and your self-righteous Indian princessing to notice."

I was noticing then. Absolutely noticing. On notice.

I heard the neglect in Shelby's words, the exhaustion, the frustration. So, no, I wasn't about to stop her to explain that there's no such thing as an Indian princess.

"You don't have real problems, Louise." Her tone turned mocking. "'Oh, no! The homecoming king can't get over me.' 'Alas, I was a raging bitch, so the hot new guy has stopped fawning all over everything I say.' Let's dissect *that* for the billionth time."

In her regular voice, Shelby added, "Do you have any idea how spoiled you are? How pampered and protected? You have everything, and you've never had to earn a dime, and don't pretend that doing household chores for your parents or babysitting your perfect little brother or playing office with your doting older cousin counts. Because it doesn't. That's fun money. Spending money. You *do whatever you want* with it.

"Meanwhile, when I finally get a few minutes to spare, you're completely blowing me off except for when you want to talk, talk, talk about yourself. You don't care about my life."

"I care," I insisted. "I . . . I've been writing that series of stories on working students."

The words sounded far weaker out loud than they had in my head.

"Well, then, nothing I'm saying matters." Shelby slid out of the booth. "By all means, go ahead and pat yourself on the back while this lowly peasant bows in gratitude." Her bow was more of a flourished curtsy, but she'd made her point.

Some jerk whistled for her attention. "Another beer!"

"Coming!" Shelby smoothed her apron, plastered on a smile, and hopped to it.

My head fell into my hands again. I was one of *those* friends.

I'd taken Shelby for granted. We still talked while she drove me to and from school. Since Joey and I had gotten serious, though, I'd skipped out on her in the cafeteria and reorganized my days to spend more time with him.

Yes, Shelby logged a lot of hours at the pub—too many. Anyone could see that.

But I hadn't really appreciated, day-to-day, how stressed she felt. After her dad covered the monthly bills and sent child support to her ex-stepmom, there was nothing left.

Shelby was completely responsible for her own out-of-pocket expenses.

For her big-ticket expenses, too.

Shelby, who'd treated me to the fancy nail salon for my birthday.

By the time she came back, my best friend had cooled down. "One question, Louise. I have to know: When you insulted Joey, his father, and—what?—*millions* of Middle Eastern people, what was happening in your perfect genius brain?"

I blinked up at her. "I was trying to communicate a quasi-parallel construct."

"Come again?" she asked.

Might as well spit it out. "I was trying to seduce him."

"You're serious." Shelby set down the beer pitcher. "Oh, God, don't cry. I can't handle crying. If you cry, I'll cry, too, and I have to work."

She bent to hug me. "I love you, Louise. I'm sorry for being a bitch and I'm sorry about Joey. He was a huge improvement over Cam."

We both started laughing, and I said, "No, you were right. What you said, I needed to hear it." I swallowed the hitch in my throat. "I'm sorry, and I love you, too."

Shelby and I had driven separately to the Grub Pub. Daddy was still in self-imposed quarantine (nobody wants a sneezing dentist), so I had his car.

All week, Hughie had put off quitting the musical. According to the schedule on our refrigerator, opening night was tomorrow and tonight was full dress. But when Hughie walked out of school that evening, he was all by himself and he wasn't wearing his Tin Man costume.

He'd finally told them he wouldn't go on with the show.

On the way home, I asked, "Estonko?"

"Here mahe." Hughie fastened his seat belt. "It wasn't terrible."

Inhaling the to-go waffle fries that I'd brought, Hughie explained that, after rehearsal, Mrs. Q had declared his announcement and his reasons for it a "teachable moment."

She'd led a discussion about the relationship

between artists and their art and their audiences. Mrs. Q said that, at first, it had been easy for her to mentally separate Baum's editorials from the Oz musical, and she admitted that she hadn't wanted to think hard about all that. But then she remembered how disappointed she'd been when one of her longtime favorite hunky movie stars had gone on a widely broadcast drunken rant and turned out to be a racist, anti-Semitic troll.

Hollywood forgave him (in the Name of All That Is Money), but, according to the Theater teacher, she could no longer watch his movies without being haunted by what he'd said.

Mrs. Q had apologized to my brother for dismissing his words so casually, and she thanked him for teaching her how to be a better educator.

"Wow!" I exclaimed. "She actually said that?"

"I know, right?" At a stoplight, Hughie concluded, "Then A.J. pointed out the whole issue of athletes and steroids, which is kind of different and kind of not. It changes the way you think about them and what they do."

Even in the theater, all roads lead to sports. Still, it was a relief that Hughie now had support from his teacher and at least one of his friends. "How about the rest of the cast and crew?"

My phone pinged. Another tornado watch notification. So far, the worst of it was light drizzle. I added, "How about Chelsea?"

"Chelsea said—*everybody* said—they understood,

but, you know. We'll see how it goes when there isn't a teacher around. After I quit, Garrett joked that I was 'off the reservation.' But he busts on everyone."

I will never understand why being a horrible human being all the time is supposed to make it less bad each time. But if Garrett or anyone else connected to the musical was behind the harassment, it should've stopped then. At least so far as Hughie and my family were concerned.

My brother wadded up the empty fry bag. "Besides, he's thrilled that I quit. Garrett got what he's wanted all along. Now he's the Tin Man."

A Cry in the Night

A faint, fuzzy whisper of the puppies barking suddenly turned high-pitched, insistent, blurring into my dreams. Then a blaring car horn fully awakened me just past three a.m.

I opened my eyes to darkness. Glass had shattered. Not in my room. On the first floor?

The house alarm wailed—loud, urgent, unrelenting.

A storm? A break-in? Was my family in danger?

No denying the dogs' distraught yelping now.

I leaped from my bed, yanked open my window, caught a glimpse of a lone figure—probably male—running toward the approaching red Porsche, its top down.

Was that Daniel's car?

The fleeing person was carrying something bulky—about the size of a garden watering can—in one hand. It banged against his thigh, slowing him down.

He intercepted the sports car in the middle of the cul-de-sac, nearly three doors up, then dropped whatever it was into the back and leaped into the front passenger seat.

The Porsche executed a sharp U-turn and peeled out in the opposite direction.

I grabbed my robe, tossed it over my nightshirt, and burst into the upstairs hall.

The lights were all on; the whole family was up.

"All clear!" Mama shouted from downstairs. "They're gone!"

A moment later, she added, "It's a can of paint!"

I remember thinking that didn't sound so bad.

"Wait for me to disable the alarm!" Daddy called. Four beeps later, he was first out the front door. Mama was on his heels, Hughie and me on hers. We shut the puppies in behind us.

The message was painted, huge, in bloody red on our garage door.

"There is no place like home."
Go back to where you came from.

I could still hear Frodo and Bilbo barking from inside.

I should've chosen full-grown dogs. A bigger, more intimidating breed.

In the driveway, Daddy swung an arm around Hughie's shoulders. "No permanent harm done," my father said, stifling a cough.

None of us could stop staring at the message. Mama drew us together, our circle of love facing down hate. "Y'all keep breathing," she said. "Every breath is a victory."

In the kitchen, Hughie and I each cradled a shaking pup. We'd all hurried back inside after realizing we'd left Bilbo and Frodo locked in with the broken window glass, but they'd apparently stayed in the foyer and would be fine once they calmed down.

The security camera had captured our skulking enemy in a ski mask and gloves, carrying the paint can in one hand and something thicker, bigger, and bulkier, in the other.

Still too hard to make out what. The light was low. It had all happened so fast.

From the video, we could tell the jerk painted the message and stuck the lid back on the can. The car horn sounded. He seemed to panic and jogged backward into our garbage bin, knocking it over. Then, apparently furious, he heaved the paint can, breaking our picture window, and sprinted away, up the street.

The Porsche never appeared in the frame.

Only I had glimpsed it speeding off.

Before long, Daddy was telling us to "Stay back!" as he cleared away the sharp fragments of glass. Mama was on the phone with the police, using words like *vandalism* and *property damage*. I thought again of Daniel — managing editor, friend. Getaway driver?

He was a white boy, a middle-class boy, a suburban boy. An athlete.

The justice system usually looked out for people

like him. I didn't trust the system, but I also wasn't sure it had been his car. Or that he'd been the one driving.

What's more, I wanted to believe the best of him. If Daniel was innocent, there was no need to drag him into this, and he might never forgive me if I falsely accused him. If I was wrong.

I had to be wrong. At school, the *Hive* was where I belonged, where I fit in.

I was in no hurry to tear that apart.

Hours later, on our way to school, I shared with Shelby most of what had happened—about the series of hate notes and the painted message, too.

The latter couldn't have been more public. I no longer saw any reason not to fill her in. Especially given the way she had gaped at the garage door when she arrived to pick me up.

Shelby was outraged. She vowed to stand by me. She vowed to kick some ass.

But Daniel was my friend, not hers. I kept my suspicions about him to myself.

Before the first bell, I waited alone for Daniel outside school. I was chilly as I leaned against the eight-foot-tall Honeybee statue at the entrance. I surveyed the steady migration of students from car pools, buses, the parking lot. The last stragglers.

Finally there he was in his letterman jacket and Iowa State ball cap.

Rubbing his eyes, Daniel nearly tripped over the fire

hydrant. Being up half the night would've made him tired. The fatigue was hitting me, too.

"Don't say anything," I said a moment later, seizing his arm. "Just come with me."

"What?" One hundred seventy pounds of solid muscle, he didn't budge. "What's up?"

"Was your dad's car stolen?" I asked. "Did I see it tear down my street—?"

"Oh, fuck," Daniel said. "I'll explain everything, Lou. But we can't talk here."

We ended up at the tennis courts that are half tucked behind the school. Private enough for our conversation but still visible from the parking lot. "I covered for you to my parents!"

"It's not what you think." Daniel opened the chain-link gate. "I was there last night to *stop* what was happening. That's why I laid on the car horn."

I followed him inside. "*After* your friend painted that message on my garage."

"*Before* he started the *fire*," Daniel replied.

"Fire?" I exclaimed. "He came to burn down my—?"

"The trash bin—or the trash inside the bin, not the house itself." Daniel set down his backpack. "At least that was the plan. He also had a can of gasoline with him. It's still in my dad's car. So's the foam paintbrush."

"It's *fire*! It could've spread! That's what fire does."

The puppies had tried to warn us, but they'd bark at shadows, at each other, at nothing at all. My family had been sound asleep until . . . until Daniel had woken us up.

I sank onto a bench. "Your friend broke a window, too. Who was it?"

"More of a teammate than a friend. He freaked, tossed the paint." Daniel sat beside me. "Pete has always had a temper. Plus he was drunk. Pete wanted to scare Hughie, and he's got some grudge against you for rejecting him, especially since Cam Ryan's been going on and on about how easy—"

"Pete?" I exclaimed. "As in Peter Ney? His mother sent him to—"

"No," Daniel said. "Honestly, I doubt she knew thing one about it. She's evil and manipulative, not evil and destructive. Mrs. Ney and her ladies who lunch, they're too dainty to do anything like that, and they'd never put their flat asses on the line, either."

I knew from Emily's story about the guy who'd threatened her dad's floral business that the grown-ups involved in PART weren't all church ladies. But otherwise, Daniel's assessment rang true.

He tightened the heavy gray scarf around his neck, adding, "Pete was on foot, super wasted. He'd been talking large to his equally wasted buddies. They'd been drinking beer all night at the new housing construction site a couple of blocks from where you live. After Pete took off on his own, one of them texted me. On Wrestling, we try to look out for each other."

It must have been interior paint, I realized. I scooted back, putting distance between us. "Whose side are you on?"

Daniel blew into his hands, rubbed them together. "I was never on their side. Not PART's. Or Pete's. Or, well, not Pete's when it came to you and your brother. Last night, I was trying to stop Pete from doing something he'd regret and—"

"Protecting your own interests?" I asked, remembering that the Wrestling coach had demanded that Daniel choose between the team and the *Hive*.

As for the rest of it, I'd already written off Peter months before. If he wanted to believe what Cam had been saying about me, fine. That was their mutual delusion.

What mattered now was my friendship with Daniel.

Assuming we'd ever really been friends at all.

"An athletic scholarship could've been my ticket to college," he said. "Or partial ticket, like Alexis's brother at Iowa State."

Daniel rose to his feet as the morning bell rang. "Fuck it! I'm not Coach's little bitch or the Neys', either." Daniel lunged at the chain-link fence, gripped and shook it, *shook it,* irate, incensed, like he'd been caged far too long.

He pushed back, threw his hands up, knocked off his ball cap.

It was over in an instant. I had no idea what to say.

Facing me, he added, "So help me, Louise, I'll fucking march straight to the principal's office right now. I'll take back everything I said—everything they told me to say—about Ms. Wilson and she'll get her job back."

Her *job*? I had a sudden flash of Daniel talking to the assistant VP, accusing our Journalism teacher of— what?—corrupting young minds? "You're the reason she's on disciplinary leave! You gave them an excuse to get rid of her. Daniel, how could—?"

"I'll put a stop to it," he insisted, shaking with emotion. "I'll do whatever I have to do to." Daniel's eyes were bloodshot, teary. "Lou, are you going to tell on me and Pete?"

Like I said, fire spreads. Telling on Daniel would jeopardize his entire future. For all I knew, he had saved my family, and I believed him when he swore to try to make amends.

Besides, it would be impossible to definitively ID Peter from the video. If Daniel's loyalties shifted, we'd be talking about the boys' word against mine.

Still, Daniel could've stopped Peter and tried to hold him in my driveway. Called the cops on his way over and asked them to hurry there.

Screw the Bro Code. Rescuing Peter from himself hadn't been Daniel's only option.

That morning, Hughie's voice had wavered when he'd asked me if I thought "the bad guys" might come back.

My family deserved to know the truth—so did the Webers and Rodríguezes.

I wanted to forgive Daniel, but I'd never been so pissed off in my whole life.

I bent to snag his ball cap from the ground and shoved it at his belly.

"See what you can do for Ms. Wilson," I replied.

Raise the Curtain

That morning, Pep had decorated the thespians' lockers the way they did for school athletes on competition days. That afternoon, my family's picture window had already been replaced. The paint was still defacing our garage. Mama had installed three more-visible cameras with signs warning that the premises were being electronically monitored.

She knocked on my open bedroom door. "Hughie has decided to go tonight to support his friends. I thought we should turn out to support him and see the show, if you're up to it."

She'd been in full TLC mode. Peanut-butter cookies—Hughie's favorite—were baking in the oven, and the aroma from the kitchen had me salivating.

At my white wicker desk, I looked up from my Rice University application. I'd buried myself in paperwork, trying not to think about Peter and Daniel and whether I was wrong to keep the truth about what they'd done to myself. With PART still on the attack, I was playing the long game, bargaining for the sake of the *Hive*. Joey and Karishma could mostly make up the difference for our managing editor/Sports reporter, but Ms. Wilson was a different story.

"Daddy's feeling better?"

"This morning, he pronounced himself fully cured," Mama replied. "I know better than to argue with the doctor." As a dentist, Daddy is sensitive about people not taking his medical background seriously.

"I'm not surprised that Hughie decided to go," I said. "But it'll be surreal for him." *Surreal* wasn't the right word. Was there a right word in English?

Maybe in Mvskoke.

"Why didn't you tell Hughie about Baum from the start?" I asked.

"Your father and I were planning to," Mama insisted. "But we weren't sure how to address his participating in the musical itself. Or if we should address it, especially once the backlash hit. At first, I . . . but then your father . . . Let's just say we're deeply blessed to all live together as a family, but we're still working out a few kinks in our new co-parenting dynamic."

She slowly shook her head. "I'm always torn between trying to fix the world for you kids and knowing when to get out of your way. But y'all are forging your paths on your own terms."

Yesterday, when Hughie told my parents he'd decided

to quit the play, they'd both hugged him and told them how proud they were. Because that's how we roll in the Wolfe family.

(He'll also probably score a new pair of overpriced sneakers out of it.)

Mama moved closer, smoothed my hair. "How's my other baby?"

Tired. We all were. We'd been rudely awakened the night before and had had a long day. Tonight Emily and Joey would be covering the musical, which probably meant he'd ignore me again. But this was about my brother and his friends, about our standing together as a family. Or at least occupying four plush chairs in the second row.

I replied, "I'm Team Hughie."

As we entered the auditorium, seats were filling fast. The controversy had generated a lot of buzz, even some coverage in the local media.

PART's petition had failed completely. Every performance had sold out.

A student usher handed me a program, and I flipped it to the back page.

Hughie's badass write-up, "Journey to Oz," talked about the various incarnations of the story and called out L. Frank Baum on his pro-genocide editorials.

What Hughie had written in his original draft had been expanded by another two paragraphs. He'd paid tribute to the Lakota lives lost and quoted Baum's own language:

The Whites, by law of conquest, by justice of civiliza-
tion, are masters of the American continent, and the best
safety of the frontier settlers will be secured by the total
annihilation of the few remaining Indians.

It hurt, reading those words again. No one could deny their brutality.

"Mrs. Q had a change of heart," Hughie explained. "She said her opinion had 'evolved.'"

I wasn't all that surprised. I'd heard Mama on the phone, talking—teacher to teacher—to Mrs. Q only a few days before.

"Brava! Bravo!" I'd lost myself in Dorothy Gale's adventure, was charmed by the choreography and swept away by the songs. The sets, the lighting—the musical had been an unabashed success. When Hughie sprang to his feet for the ovation, I stood to applaud his friends, too. It pained me to think that PART would assume it had defeated him somehow.

If it had been me in Hughie's fake tin shoes, I can't say for sure what I would have done.

Yes, knowing about Baum had tainted Oz for me, too. But under the circumstances, for Chelsea and A.J. and even for Mrs. Q, I might've made the decision to go on with the show.

Would I have done it to spite PART?

Maybe.

Out of love for performing?

I can't say. I don't have an actor's passion for theater.

What I do know without a doubt is that Hughie would've been ten times the Tin Man of that loser Garrett. My brother has the biggest heart of anyone I know.

By the way, Garrett's understudy, Marissa Berry, had moved into his original role when he took over for Hughie. Mrs. Q had played the cast shuffle close to the vest.

Some people in the audience gasped when they realized the Wizard was a girl.

Hughie had the cast party to go to, and I'd told our parents I could catch a ride home with a friend. After the second curtain call, Emily and Joey found us in the jovial crowd exiting the auditorium. It was the first time he and I had been face-to-face since my epic relationship fail.

Joey said hi to Hughie, not me.

"Why didn't you go on tonight?" Emily asked my brother. "What about the rest of the performances this weekend?"

"Want to interview me for the *Hive*?" Hughie offered with unexpected enthusiasm.

"I thought I already was," she replied. That's when Emily seemed to realize he had something big to say. "Let's set up the shoot onstage," she suggested, and they did.

Maybe I should've given Emily a heads-up once Hughie had announced his decision at rehearsal. But my first loyalty was to my brother, and it honestly hadn't occurred to me that he'd want—let alone be eager—to speak out publicly.

As Joey checked the frame and audio levels, I pulled Hughie to the left wing, behind the drawn red-velour curtain. "You don't have to do this," I said. "You don't owe anybody an explanation. Emily's my friend. She'll understand if you—"

"I know what I'm doing," Hughie assured me.

When Emily asked him to explain himself, actor Hughie Wolfe opened with the words "Tonight's show rocked." My brother had taken center stage like it belonged to him. Like he was born to stand there. Hughie went on to identify himself as a Muscogee Nation citizen. He explained about L. Frank Baum's editorials and the atrocity at Wounded Knee.

Hughie read out loud for the camera what he'd written for the musical program.

"Baum created the Tin Man," he added. "That ruined the role for me. I tried, but I couldn't get past it. I kept forgetting my lines. I kept missing my cues. It could've compromised my performance, and that wouldn't have been fair to the rest of the cast and crew."

Hughie spread his arms wide in front of the Kansas backdrop. The painted sunflowers. The make-do farmhouse. The papier-mâché brown cows.

"Let me be clear: I didn't quit the musical because of Parents Against Revisionist Theater. I won a major role, fair and square.

"I had every right to play the Tin Man, just like I had every right not to."

"Thanks, Hughie," Emily said. "This is Emily Bennett for the *Hive,* reporting with Joseph A. Kairouz, on opening night of *The Wizard of Oz.*"

Hughie had had his moment in the spotlight after all.

Lower the Curtain

As Hughie hurried backstage to congratulate his friends, I heard Emily say to Joey that they'd better get moving to catch the actors still in makeup and costume.

"Joey!" Always the optimist, I called after him from center stage. "Can I get a ride when you're done?" When he didn't respond, I decided to push the issue. "You can't avoid me forever. We're still both assigned to Features. We need to talk."

"Alas, I'm busy doing a Features story right now," Joey replied, marching up the orange-carpeted aisle without so much as a backward glance. "Good night, Ms. Wolfe."

Smart-ass. Fine, I'd tried. And tried and tried.

What else could I do? My fault, but, wow, he was stubborn.

Didn't I—doesn't everyone—deserve a second chance?

This was nothing more than a misunderstanding. The way I saw it, Joey was being unreasonable. Self-righteous. Holier than thou.

Why wouldn't he hear me out? I was a good person. So, I'd misspoken—big deal.

I'd said one damn random little thing. . . .

I caught myself up short. That thought hadn't sounded like mine.

Where had it come from? The words floated up from my memory: *"I say any damn random little thing that pisses you off . . . "* Holy crap, I was the *Cam Ryan* in this situation!

Joey and I were over because I'd been an asshole.

Ping! Emily had texted to offer me a ride home when she was done.

While I was waiting, Cam's new girlfriend, Hannah, came up to me. I was in line for a pod of water at the concession window, and I almost didn't recognize her out of a JV Cheer uniform.

She got right to the point. "Here's the thing: Cam needs closure. Or at least I need for Cam to have closure. I definitely need him to stop talking about you all the time. He says you two had a 'special place.' Will you meet him there on Monday after school?"

Of course Cam was talking about me all the time to make her jealous. No mystery there, and not my problem, either. But Hannah looked so sincere, hopeful. Like she'd rather be pulling out her own teeth than having our conversation. I said, "I'll think about it."

In the school parking lot, Emily pulled on her helmet, grabbed the handlebars of her middle brother's motorcycle, and swung her leg over the leather seat. She'd forgone her usual long dresses to wear pants for the occasion. "Hop on, Lady Lou. I'll have you home in no time."

The temperature was about 30 degrees, not that I was complaining.

"Try not to kill us," I said, holding on to Emily's waist. "Should I be wearing a helmet?"

"You bet!" she called as the bike's engine roared to life.

Posturing aside, Emily wasn't homicidal. She basically puttered toward my house.

"How long have you and Rebecca been friends?" I asked, leaning close to her ear.

"We're *girl*friends, not *just* friends," Emily shouted. "December will be our six-month anniversary. We're going ice-skating at Crown Center in Kansas City."

We bounced over a speed bump. "Congratulations!"

I tightened my grip a little. "I didn't realize you two were a couple."

I thought about it. "I'm so glad you're a couple!"

I thought about it more. "Skating sounds really romantic."

Emily cruised into my subdivision. "You're wondering about me and Kyle Rittmaster."

No, I wasn't. "I have no idea who you're talking about."

I was shivering. Christmas decorations weren't even up yet, and I could see my breath. We passed the Emerald Hills pool and clubhouse. The air smelled rain fresh.

Emily said, "Kyle and I went out for most of junior year so . . ."

"So, you date boys and girls," I said, realizing from the way she'd brought it up that not everybody had been supportive. It meant a lot that she'd felt safe enough to tell me.

"I've dated *a* boy and *a* girl," she clarified, turning the bike. "But theoretically, yes, Lady Lou. Becs only dates girls, though. Only dates *me.*"

Emily sounded delighted by that, and I was honored to be in the know.

"What's this drama with you and Joey?" she asked, turning onto my cul-de-sac.

"He's furious. Won't talk to me. It's your standard living-hell situation."

"I noticed the pitchforks and bonfires," Emily replied. "What happened?"

"I said something horrible that I didn't mean." (I know, understatement.)

Emily pulled into my driveway and I climbed off the bike.

"Look, I've got three brothers," she said. "If a guy . . . Make that *most* guys. If most guys are lonely, they act mad. If they're insecure, they act mad. If they're freaking out or jealous or in over their heads or whatever . . ."

For the time being, Daddy had hung a large plastic sheet over the garage door. If Emily noticed, she didn't mention it. Instead, she took off the helmet and hooked it on the handlebar.

"Most guys think that the only negative emotion they're allowed to feel is anger. If they're pissed, they're still being men. But if they show that they're sad or, God forbid, they cry, that's the worst thing they can do. According to my father."

She sounded vaguely exasperated. "Especially if you're a florist."

"Well, that sucks," I replied. It didn't bode well for my relationship with Joey, either.

"Hang in there, Lady Lou." Emily hugged me. "Everybody fucks up sometimes."

Regrets

It was Monday morning of what promised to be a stormy Thanksgiving week. I'd been one of the first students through the EHHS front doors. I'd hurried to Joey's orange locker, slipped my folded letter inside, and hovered near the corner at the end of the senior hall to watch his reaction.

> *Dear Joey,*
> *I'm sorry for what I said on the porch. I wasn't thinking clearly then, but I am now.*
>
> *Thank you for pointing out what a jackass I was. It won't happen again.*
>
> *I'll be braver and explain what's really on my mind.*
>
> *I really want to talk you in person. Please give me a chance. I swear, what you took away*

from the conversation and what I was trying to get across—farthest thing.

So I completely, hugely apologize for screwing up but not for thinking what you think I think because I don't think that. I would never think that. I already know better than to think that.

I was nervous. I babbled. I do that when I'm nervous.

What I said or was trying to say—I was babble, babble, babbling, a gushing waterfall of babbles. The freaking Niagara Falls of babbles, but I had good intentions, great intentions—mega flattering intentions, FYI, since this is a full-disclosure situation.

Not that my intentions matter more than you do. Or that you should have to listen.

But I'm not some random asshole. You and me, we were good together. Great together. So maybe you want to know what went wrong.

You may be wondering, for example, why did I go full-on babble-head?

Maybe because sex is what put me on the road to babble hell.

Well, not only sex. More like a swirling storm of debris.

Swaths that blindside, bruise, divide. Shards tearing into lungs.

You know how it goes. Day after day, we live our lives. When the breeze turns mean, we shut *our eyes, fuse our lips, but sooner or later, we dare to breathe.*

We have no choice. We crave air, however polluted, to keep our hearts beating, to give them voice. In their brum, brum, brum, brum, *that's where our hope thrives.*

This isn't an excuse. It's the beginning of an apology, an explanation, an apologetic explanation. Is there a difference, Joey?

I hate people like me sometimes.

Your (Hopefully Not) Ex-Girlfriend,

Louise

I'd labored over those words. Fretted and sweated and pinned my heart on them. I'd researched how to apologize and revised six times. It was an A apology, I was sure of it.

Okay, maybe A-/B+ on account of pushiness and self-centeredness.

(Yes, Shelby had really got me thinking.)

Joey unfolded the paper, flicked his gaze to my signature. Without hesitation, without reading a word I'd written, he ripped my letter into two pieces, then four.

They fluttered, like so much trash, to the institutional tile floor.

#ndn

When the first bell rang in Journalism, we were missing Joey, Daniel, and, most notably, Mrs. Powell, the sub. "Looks like we're on our own," Karishma said.

Without bothering to ask permission, the editors had decided to crash a special holiday edition to run the next day. Otherwise, our musical coverage—*the* story of the year—would be old news by the next scheduled publication date a week from that Friday.

"Not so fast," Ms. Wilson called, making her grand entrance with the managing editor. She had a long cardboard tube tucked under her arm.

Karishma opened her mouth to say something, but our teacher cut her off.

"Back to work," Ms. Wilson said. "Don't forget the rules."

She held up a finger. "Don't bother me unless you're on fire."

She held up another finger, and we all chimed in to add, "Don't catch on fire."

The newsroom erupted in cheers and applause, hugs and high-fives.

An overjoyed Karishma wiped away a stray tear, and I pretended not to notice. It couldn't be easy, having to be the strong one all the time.

With a flourish, Daniel ripped the *Honeybee Pride* poster off the bulletin board and turned to Ms. Wilson. "Can I give you a hand with that?" he asked.

Together, they hung a new First Amendment poster in its rightful place.

"Cut the feather," Karishma said a half hour later. "Otherwise, it's good to go."

"Without the feather, how are readers going to know?" Nick countered from his desk in the far left-hand corner of the newsroom. He pointed at her. "Dot." Then at me. "Feather."

The editor in chief didn't bother scolding him. "We're running the video interview with Hughie in the same issue as the musical coverage. People should be able to figure it out."

"Can I take a look?" I asked. Technically, it wasn't my place to get involved, both because the musical had been partly my beat and because of the focus on Hughie.

Karishma waved me over anyway, and then Alexis slowly rose from her desk and walked up behind us, too.

On Nick's screen, his latest editorial cartoon depicted Hughie in a T-shirt and jeans with an upright feather in his hair. He was facing off—like a fighter in a boxing ring—against a wizard sporting a pointy dunce (wizard-style) cap, vertically labeled B-A-U-M.

Meanwhile, Ms. Wilson was pretending not to eaves-drop. Emily was doing a phone interview. Joey was still "out on assignment." Or hiding. For all I knew, he was just hiding.

A copy of *The Wonderful Wizard of Oz,* tabbed in two places, rested on Nick's desk.

I bent to read over one of his shoulders. Alexis bent over the other one.

In the cartoon, the Baum-Wizard's speech bubble read:

> *If I should go out of this Palace my people would soon discover I am not a Wizard, and then they would be vexed with me for having deceived them.*

Hughie's speech bubble countered: *I think you are a very bad man.*

"Enough hovering," Nick said, glancing over each of his shoulders in turn.

"The wizard quote is long," Alexis put in as we both stepped back. "It's crowding the illustration, making it too gray."

"Besides, hasn't Baum said enough?" I added.

Karishma and Nick exchanged a meaningful look. He double-clicked and deleted the Baum-Wizard's words, the speech bubble that had framed them, and then the feather.

I hated to admit it, but Nick kind of had a point. Anyone who hadn't watched Emily's interview with Hughie probably wouldn't understand the editorial cartoon.

"Do you mind?" I asked, gesturing to the keyboard.

Nick moved his wheelchair, giving me room to type.

To cartoon Hughie's T-shirt, I added *#NDN*.

Call it a compromise. A clue. Readers could click to learn more.

Once the editorial cartoon was finalized, Nick said, "Lou, I heard about your fight with Cam over the spirit signs. I, uh, helped make one of them. I drew the . . ."

He paused, collected his thoughts. "I didn't realize it would upset anybody."

Sting the Braves! "Yeah, I figured. Thanks for taking it down."

"I didn't," Nick replied. "I mean, I would've. Because we're friends and it was god-awful and Cam Ryan is a total douche." I could tell Nick longed to say more about the mascot cartoon but wasn't sure of his words. Instead, he assured me again, "I would've ripped it down, but somebody beat me to it."

Small Victories

Alongside his nana's retirement complex pool, Cam and I were both dressed in layers. Bundled up. He was in his letterman jacket.

This had been our place, a semiprivate getaway, in the weeks leading up to junior prom. Somewhere we could go to unwind and splash in soaking wet, skimpy swimwear.

I shivered in the icy mist. "You know, that day on the bridge when we argued about the spirit signs?" I began. "Later, somebody tore them down. Was it you?"

"Hannah," Cam said. "She thought about what you said."

As of that moment, I officially liked Hannah. So far as I was concerned, she belonged at the top of the JV Cheer pyramid.

"I could have practically any girl in school." Cam snapped his fingers. "Like that. I don't know why I keep going for girls who're so uptight."

As he dragged a couple of lounge chairs closer together, it occurred to me that, maybe, despite noises to the contrary, Cam had more respect for girls who didn't automatically defer to him. On the other hand, I still didn't appreciate what he'd said about me being a "crazy nympho." I wouldn't have shown up at all if I hadn't been so curious about the spirit signs.

But now, looking at Cam in the letterman jacket I'd once been so proud to wear, the memories of our good times outweighed the bad. And after the way I'd screwed up with Joey, I was in a more forgiving mood.

I set down my bead-accented purse and lowered myself onto a chair, careful not to tip it. Hannah had been the one who'd asked for this meeting. What did closure mean to *Cam*?

"I'm sorry I broke up with you that way," I said. "We should've talked in person."

Nothing would change the fact that Cam had been my first real boyfriend. I wanted to make peace with him and with that fading part of myself.

"If it makes you feel any better, Joey dumped me."

The pool had been drained for winter and covered with a tarp. Without the scent of chlorine and sparkly moonlit water, this place had lost its magic.

"It doesn't make me feel better," Cam said, cracking his knuckles. "Kairouz dumped *my* ex-girlfriend? That's bullshit. Loulou, you're way out of his league."

Was it wrong that some small part of me appreciated Cam for saying that?

"Joey just stopped speaking to me." I shot Cam a look. "He didn't even send an e-mail."

That earned me a reluctant grin. Cam took off his jacket and wrapped it backward around me. I let him. He was trying to be considerate, and I was freaking freezing.

Neither of us seemed sure where to take the conversation from there.

Cam and I had gone out for months. We should've had more to say to each other.

"You and Hannah make a cute couple," I finally ventured. He towered over her, but it was still true. And, thankfully, she wasn't some wide-eyed, starstruck freshman.

"She's incredibly hot," Cam needlessly reminded me. "But I never would've dated Hannah if I hadn't known you. You're the reason that I like smart girls."

It was his version of a non-apology apology.

"Thanks." I'd take my victories where I could get them.

Courage

An hour before school, Karishma brought me a cup of hot tea in the newsroom. "I'm not trying to rush you," she began. "But Alexis has already filed the story for News."

What with the musical successfully behind us and the public nature of the graffiti on my garage door, the affected families had all green-lighted my going public.

I seized the opportunity to make what had happened the topic of my editorial, but I felt like I was failing everybody. Especially Hughie.

My laptop screen was blank. I'd started and deleted three drafts.

Karishma added, "If you want your tie-in editorial to run today . . ."

"I do—I really do." I took a sip. "But whenever I start typing, I get pissed off and can't think what to say and I freeze up because I feel like I have to be hyper-rational so I don't come off like some self-indulgent, fragile flower. . . ." I shook my head. "How do you do this every week?"

Karishma reached toward the screen as if to touch the image of my defaced garage and then drew her hand away. "The more the topic hits home, the harder it—"

"Home," I whispered.

THE HIVE

OPINION: WELCOME HOME TO EAST HANNESBURG HIGH

by Louise M. Wolfe, *Hive* staff

7:32 a.m. CT, Tuesday, November 24

It's not hard to read between these two lines.

> *"There is no place like home."*
> Go back to where you came from.

Senior Chelsea Weber is Black. Junior A.J. Rodríguez is Latino, Mexican American. Freshman Hughie Wolfe is Native, a citizen of the Muscogee Nation. They also are the first-ever nonwhite students to win starring roles on the EHHS stage. Though Wolfe didn't perform, they were all originally cast in last weekend's production of *The Wizard of Oz*.

In response, hateful, anonymous notes were slipped into their school lockers and residential mailboxes. Being Hughie's sister, I received one in my locker, too.

A final message was painted in red on the Wolfe family's garage at approximately three a.m. on the day of the first performance. The perpetrator also shattered a large window.

Was it the symbolism? Intentional or not, casting those

three students as a Kansas girl and farmhands in a story centered on the concept of *home* sent a strong message. Even given the fantastical personas the boys would take on when the action moved to Oz itself.

Somebody decided to target them and their families because of it.

Why? Because of the assumption that only white people are owed the spotlight?

Because of the belief—as the messages suggest—that those particular student actors somehow can't already be at home in Kansas?

This kind of harassment is sweeping the United States. Descendants of immigrants are lashing out against newcomers and people of color and citizens of Indigenous nations.

It's happening right here at EHHS.

Maybe you're thinking that's terrible but it has nothing to do with you. You'd never send hate mail or vandalize someone's house. You'd never threaten anyone.

But behavior like that doesn't come out of nowhere. It's fueled every time we ignore or excuse or explain away bigoted words and actions. Those that are obvious and blatant, those that are small and subtle, yet evermore destructive in their cumulative effect.

It's fueled every time we minimize each other's perspective or lived experience. Every time we presume to judge—to approve or dismiss—pain or a perspective outside our own.

Yes, we all make mistakes. Recently, I made a couple

of huge mistakes and hurt people who are precious to me. I am sorry. I'm working to make amends and do better.

We can all do better.

Let's take responsibility.

Let's welcome each other home.

THE HIVE

LETTERS TO THE EDITOR

2:15 p.m. CT, Tuesday, November 24

It's a pain in the ass that the Wolfe family has to repaint their garage, but I don't see what the big deal is otherwise. So not everyone loves you. Get over it.

—Neal Miller, junior

On behalf of the Honeybees defensive line, if anyone tries to mess with my ex-girlfriend, her little brother, or his friends again, you will have to answer to us.

—Cam Ryan, senior

First, I want to personally express my solidarity with the Theater students and their families and my condemnation of the attacks on their peace of mind and the Wolfes' property.

Please know that many teachers are regarding this as a wake-up call to better educate our students throughout the curriculum.

—Jonah McCloud, teacher

Until now, only my closest friends here knew it, but I am a citizen of the Prairie Band Potawatomi. I am proud that Hughie Wolfe is representing Native people in Theater. I hope to see him onstage this spring and in years to come.
—**Buffy Mitchell, sophomore**

Faith Renewed

Shelby had decided that starting at a four-year university wasn't her only option. On Wednesday, school was out and the Grub Pub had already shut down for the Thanksgiving holiday weekend. We took advantage of the opportunity to road-trip to Johnson County Community College in Overland Park. It's a sprawling campus of redbrick buildings, lots of green grass, and lots of parking lots. Moneyed. Close enough to East Hannesburg that Shelby could potentially live at home, keep her waitressing job, and commute to school two or three days a week.

Classes weren't in session. The offices were closed. But it's one thing to check out a place on the web, another to walk around. We started at the Carlsen Center and went from there.

"It's still expensive, but I might be able to swing it," my best friend said afterward, driving home in the light rain on Kansas Highway 10.

She'd cleared out the trash from the floorboards of her dad's station wagon and hung a vanilla-scented, leaf-shaped air freshener from the rearview mirror. To either side of the road, cornfields and hay bales peeked between autumn trees. A prominent sign advertised land for sale.

"I have to admit, I'm jealous that you automatically get college for free." Shelby hit her turn signal and moved into the fast lane. "You know, on account of your being Indian."

I turned down the vein-removal ad on the radio. "I don't automatically get college for free," I said. "I'm applying for a tribal funds grant along with other grants and scholarships for Native applicants and for veterans' kids and for people in my range of kick-booty test scores who've taken AP classes practically since preschool and haven't gotten a B since — watch out!"

Shelby swerved, blasting her car horn at the hatchback that had drifted into our lane.

"That wasn't my fault!" she exclaimed. "That was its fault!"

"Her fault," I specified, having a better view of the driver from the passenger side. I elected not to mention that she was probably cussing us out and definitely giving us the finger.

"Not your fault," I agreed. "You're doing terrific. Breathe and drive. Drive and breathe."

Traffic had thickened considerably. The roads threatened to ice over.

"Driving," Shelby said. "Breathing." She checked her rearview mirror and slowed to put more distance between us and the hatchback. After it exited, she asked, "You got a B?"

"Seventh-grade Gym," I admitted.

Shelby switched to a radio station already playing Christmas music. "Gym?"

"I served a volleyball directly into Mrs. Garcia's head."

Shelby was trying not to laugh. "She teaches Phys Ed. She should've blocked it."

Mrs. Garcia had been making a note on her clipboard at the time, but I appreciated my best friend taking my side. "Valid point," I told Shelby. "She should've blocked it."

Family dinner was delivery barbecue at my cousins' house to welcome home their dad, who was on leave from Andersen Air Force Base in Guam.

Then we all went to the Wednesday night service at First Baptist in old town. It's not like church in Oklahoma, with our grands, our greats, our aunties and uncles, our countless more cousins. But Mama brings a Mvskoke Bible, and we make do.

The gratitude service had drawn a full house, so Rain and I ended up sitting on the thinly padded wooden pew behind the rest of the family. "Louise," she whispered, "at Bierfest, when you didn't come back right away from walking Joey to his Jeep, I went looking for you."

I had a wispy memory of a text from her, asking if I was okay. "I shut off my phone."

"I figured. I spotted you two, realized you were fine," Rain said. "Better than fine."

I hadn't told her about the breakup yet. I was trying (and failing) not to think about it.

She added, "I took one shot, for your eyes only. And Joey's, I guess, if you want to forward it to him. I'd forgotten all about it until today when I was showing pics to my dad."

The pastor welcomed the congregation, and we shushed. Rain slipped her phone onto her lap, shielding it with one hand. Making sure mine was on mute, I did the same.

Mama's rule is "No phone during church."

Daddy's rule is "No phone during church unless it's silent and no adult sees you."

I studied Rain's sun-drenched image of Joey and me kissing. I could almost taste the spice on his full lips and hear the oompah music playing in the distance.

One last time, I decided. One last show of faith. I'd try again to finish what I'd started to say on my front porch. If Joey wouldn't listen, there was nothing more I could do.

I owed him an apology. He didn't owe me anything.

The pastor directed us to Psalm 107:

O give thanks unto the Lord; for He is good;
for His mercy endureth for ever.

That night, after putting on my flannel pj's and climbing into bed, I received a text from Daniel, asking if I would be willing to cover the Turkey Trot the next day.

Seizing the opportunity, I wrote back: *Only IF J videos it.*

Before our breakup, Joey had mentioned that his sister had decided to stay at K-State to study (or maintain her denial about their parents' divorce) and that he would be at his mom's for Thanksgiving. Since there was no point in roasting a whole turkey for only two people, they'd planned to have dinner at Applebee's. He'd be in East Hannesburg tomorrow for sure.

An excruciating hour and a half later, my phone rang. "Joey will meet you tomorrow morning at the race," the managing editor told me. "But he's not happy about it."

After I thanked him, Daniel said, "By the way, I met with Pastor Ney in his office and told him everything. He's not his wife. Not that he was oblivious to PART or, for that matter, her personality. But I don't think he fully realized—"

"Daniel!" I pushed away my comforter. "By 'everything,' you mean . . . ?"

"Everything I know about the 'go back to where you came from' notes, the broken window, and painted message on your garage, how Coach said I had to choose between Wrestling and the *Hive*. Everything except that *you* know who's behind it all, too."

My mixed feelings aside, I knew Daniel appreciated that I'd kept his secret.

He added, "I told Pastor Ney that Pete could've been arrested, probably *would've* been arrested if I hadn't shown up, and that Pete gets bat-shit out-of-control when he drinks. Then I told the pastor about the can of gasoline."

"About the hate mail," I began, "do you know—?"

"I'm still not clear on whether that was all Pete or if his mom put him up to it. Believe me, he resents the hell out of her, too. Pete's miserable and he's looking for a place to put it."

I could hear in Daniel's voice that he felt sorry for Peter.

"What did the pastor say?" I asked. "Did he believe you?"

After all, we were talking about the man's wife and kid.

"He did after I used my phone to play my conversation with Pete from that night in the car." Smart. Daniel had recorded them talking, like we did with interviews for the *Hive*.

He added, "Besides, when I'd dropped Pete off, I got the feeling that wasn't the first time he had come home wasted or had blown his curfew on a school night.

"Then Pastor Ney thanked me. He said I've been a good friend to his son and that the Immanuel Baptist family needs more fine young Christian men like me."

Couldn't argue with that, but . . . "Are you going back to church there?" I asked.

"No way in hell," Daniel said.

Turkey Trot

When Mama and I stepped outside on that sunny Thanksgiving morning, Daddy and Hughie were clearing fallen leaves from the Shire and installing miniature ceramic turkey figurines beside each round door. Because hobbits love to eat and so do we.

Running lines together was their new father-son bonding activity. Turned out Daddy had helped Hughie prep for his post-musical statement for the *Hive,* too.

But there was still plenty of Tolkien love between them.

Carrying cvtv hakv and Watergate salad, Mama patted Daddy's shoulder. "We'd best get going." Then Hughie ran back inside to fetch the yapping puppies in their carriers.

The plan was for my family to drop me off at the city-mall complex for the Turkey Trot. They would continue to my cousins' house to help prepare the meal.

After finishing my Journalism assignment, I'd call for a ride and join them all for dinner.

My grandparents and great-auntie had planned to drive up, but massive thunderstorms were rolling across Oklahoma. We'd had rain showers here in Kansas off and on for days. So Daddy had delayed painting over Peter's graffiti because of all the moisture in the air.

On the upside, word of what had happened had spread quickly on the cul-de-sac. My family had taken comfort in an outpouring of support from our neighbors, many of whom had sent thinking-of-you cards or personally delivered casseroles.

We even received a potted white peace lily from the homeowners' association.

The Turkey Trot is a 5K run, a soup-kitchen fund-raiser, and an opportunity to burn off calories in anticipation of the Thanksgiving feast. It felt like the whole town had turned out.

I was heartened to spot Emily and Rebecca, daring to hold hands in public. A bold move for Emily, but huge for Rebecca. Today she wasn't hiding behind her hair.

Waving, I scanned the people around them. Nobody else seemed to take notice, at least not in a bad way, and I silently prayed that would hold throughout the event.

Cam's mother jogged up to me. "Happy Thanksgiving, Louise!"

She had on a race T-shirt and an orange headband. "How are you, dear?"

Before I could reply, she added, "Do you happen to

know Cam's new friend Hannah? Do you think she's a nice girl?"

I thought it would do wonders for Cam if his mother stopped treating him like a pampered prince. "I don't know Hannah well, but I like what I do know. She's a strong enough cheerleader to have been competitive in Texas."

So far as Mrs. Ryan was concerned, it was the highest praise I could give.

She'd be quoting me on that.

Nearby, Cam was pinning on his race number, and his dad was pointing out a middle-aged man in a turkey costume. Talk about holiday spirit.

"Oh, forgive me, Louise!" Mrs. Ryan exclaimed. "I didn't think. You poor thing. Surely, it can't be easy for you, seeing Cam with another girl."

I did my best to maintain a polite smile. "I persevere. Is Cam's brother running today?"

"He's with his fiancée's family," she said. "But the Turkey Trot is becoming a Ryan holiday tradition. I fully expect the newlyweds and my darling grandbaby to join us next year."

I noticed how positive she sounded about that. "Your darling grandbaby?"

In textbook grandmotherly style, she immediately fished her phone out of her fanny pack and began scrolling through endless photos of baby Nolan who — as it turned out — was her grandson. Her biological Kickapoo grandson.

Mrs. Ryan was bursting with pride. She even bragged about how her future daughter-in-law, Laurel, had completed her education degree at KU and was in her first year of teaching elementary school in Baldwin City.

Yeah, I wished Mrs. Ryan had been equally welcoming last spring back when she viewed Laurel exclusively as a single Native mom and barista. Before she'd found out the baby was Andrew's. But in my own family, the love of little ones has worked miracles.

I smiled at the adorable photos. "Grandmothers are one of life's greatest blessings," I said, hoping to nudge her in all the right directions. "Congratulations."

She gave me one of her stiff-arm half hugs. "Happy Thanksgiving, dear."

I half hugged her back and answered, "Bless your heart."

As Mrs. Ryan disappeared into the crowd, Joey found me. "Let's get this over with."

"Did you read my editorial?" I asked.

He'd skipped Journalism on Monday and hadn't shown up Tuesday at school at all.

"No, Louise." His voice was clipped. "It wasn't on the top of my to-do list."

The national anthem played. The announcer began the countdown.

"Start talking," Joey said, making a half-assed effort to position his camera.

"This way!" I wove through waiting runners, undeterred by his lack of enthusiasm.

I did feel guilty about tricking him into hearing me out. And I'd still have to turn in the story about the race for the *Hive*. But I was desperate. If we'd knocked out our assignment first, Joey would've bailed immediately afterward. False pretenses was the only way to go.

"Where're you going?" he called, plainly losing patience.

I gestured for him to follow. "We should get creative with the shot. I want you to record me reporting from the middle of the race itself. It'll give viewers the feeling of being here."

When the starting pistol fired, I ran ahead for a minute.

Then I turned, planting myself in the center of the route.

Here they came: Runners, joggers, family teams. Over a dozen dogs on leashes.

Countless strollers. A red toy wagon. One potbellied pig.

Joey and I faced each other. He knelt as low as he could. "I'll keep the lens zoomed wide," he said. "That'll get as many racers and their shoes into the frame as possible."

He was there under protest, but he'd resigned himself to doing his usual best.

The over-sixty ladies social club that frequented the pub was power-walking in matching rainbow tutus. They briefly split into two groups to navigate around us.

That's when I spotted them, picking up the pace — the Thanksgiving enthusiasts who'd decided to have some real fun with the theme.

"Ready, Joey?"

He double-checked the sound. "I've been ready for a while, Lou."

"This is the twenty-first century," I said. "I'm a Muscogee girl—a Native girl—living here in suburban northeast Kansas. I should be able to skip along, singing a song, trying to survive high school without fakey-feather-headed redfacers swooping down like flying monkeys on national holidays and at ball games. But they do—they swoop—and sometimes it's hard for me to talk about all that."

Illustrating my point, the guy in the turkey costume jogged by, playfully chased by a guy in a Pilgrim costume wielding a plastic butcher knife, who, in turn, was playfully chased by a guy in a Hollywood Indian costume wielding a plastic tomahawk.

All around us, people—families, kids—were laughing and taking photos of them, photos with them.

"Yeah, Joey, I know what Arab Americans go through isn't the exact same thing."

At that moment, he clearly realized that what I had to say was personal.

Joey lowered the camera, closing the distance between us. "What are you doing?"

"I'm apologizing," I said. "Joey, I'm sorry. I'm sorry that I hurt you. I'm sorry that I pissed you off.

"What I was *trying* to tell you that day is that I'm Native, so having to constantly deal with other's people's ignorant bullshit is something we have in common."

I gestured at the millennials jogging by with their shih tzu decked out in a fringed costume, complete with little snap-on feather headdress. "For example!"

With a scowl, Joey took a moment to pack his

camera. Runners still streaming around us, he said, "You knew there would be people here today in feathers and face paint?"

There were more approaching in the crowd. "Yeah."

"You moved here late last December." He sounded puzzled. "You weren't at the Turkey Trot last year."

"Yeah," I replied again. "But there's one just like it—only bigger—in Austin."

Was that thunder in the distance?

The sky had turned thick and yellow.

"You know, your brother's not the only one with a theatrical streak." Joey put one arm around me and held the other out to signal *stop* to the approaching trotters, so we could exit to the sidelines. "Everything was fine," he insisted. "That day, raking leaves with the puppies, we were fine. Solid. Happy. Until you started talking about . . ."

He accepted a three-ounce paper cup from a volunteer and handed it to me. "Why on earth did you want to say all that? What the hell's going on?"

"Well, basically"—I downed the water in one gulp—"I didn't want to have sex with you and find out the next day that you're prejudiced against Native people."

He clenched his hair with both hands. "We're having *sex* now?"

"Don't get ahead of yourself," I scolded.

"Me?" he exclaimed. "*I'm* getting ahead of *myself*?"

That's when the tornado sirens went ballistic.

Whirlwind Romance

Hotvle rakko—I could see it! Overhead, a charcoal-gray funnel menaced from the west.

Not a magical, musical, carousel-like portal but a raging wind monster.

I wasn't the only one who'd spotted it. The orderly flow of Turkey Trotters broke into chaos. "Emily!" I called. "Rebecca!" No use. They'd never hear me.

The closest place to take shelter would be within the outdoor mall. But most of the shops didn't open until ten a.m., assuming they'd open at all on Thanksgiving. The two breakfast restaurants were dicey strategic choices, heavy on glass windows and glass walls.

Joey and I reached for each other's hands. The early shows at the dine-in movie theater had already begun. I could sense the flock calculating, choosing it for shelter.

A pebble struck my shoulder, another the top of my head.

Not pebbles. "Hail!"

Joey asked, "Do you trust me?"

I did. His fingers threading mine, we sprinted as fast as we could, deeper into storm, past the yogurt shop and the bouncy-ball pit. Toward the twister.

A sudden downpour of rain slicked the gold-brick walkways.

The hail grew from pebble-size to dime size.

Picking up the pace, I wished I'd never let Emily and Rebecca out of my sight.

Had the tornado touched down in old town? Was my family safe? Shelby?

What about my house? Oh, hell, the Headbirds weren't supposed to move out of their trailer until the following week.

I yelled, "Where're we going?"

"My Jeep!" Joey shouted.

I knew damn well not to take refuge in any vehicle. But Joey hadn't left it out in the open. He'd scored a spot inside the concrete parking garage. Once beneath its cover, we escaped the ferocious wind, the rain and pelting ice.

But that wasn't good enough. I sprinted after him to the Jeep and climbed inside. Then Joey drove us to the underground level and parked again.

"What am I doing?" He reached for the door handle. "I should be out there, filming—"

I grabbed his chin, turned his face toward mine. "If you get out of this car, so help me, Joseph A. Kairouz, I will never forgive you. *Never.*"

It was vexing how amused he looked when confronted by the full force of my ferocity.

"Sorry," he replied. "I didn't mean to freak you out."

While he pouted about being stuck inside *alive*, I checked my phone.

Mama had sent a family selfie (dogs and all) from my cousins' basement, begging to know where I was, if I was okay. I texted one word in reply: *Safe*.

Another *ping!* Another photo. The Headbird family was with them; Dmitri and Marie were making funny faces in the upturned flashlight beam.

Ping! Shelby was at home with her dad, playing poker by candlelight.

Apparently, both old town and East Hannesburg had lost electricity.

My thumbs flying, I texted Emily.

Ping! She and Rebecca were holed up in the ladies' room at Eggcellent Morning Café.

Brightening, Joey reached to cradle my hands. "This is better."

"Are *we* better?" I angled my lips toward his. "Are you still—?"

His kiss answered my question. His tongue erased lingering doubts.

I slid my hands up the back of his T-shirt, broke contact long enough to slip it over his wet hair. Then he returned the favor.

His mouth was grazing my shoulder when I unbuttoned the top of his waistband.

So perfect, so passionate, except . . . have you ever

tried to get busy in bucket seats or wiggle out of wet jeans in a Jeep?

It takes concentration and once the denim is past your booty, you have to shove it down your thighs. Honestly, it would be easier to get the hell out of the car, only that busts the whole über-romantic life-or-death scenario.

And then your boyfriend says, "I don't have a condom." But he slips two fingers into the front of your panties. "Do you?"

It was oh so hard to concentrate with him doing that. "No, but do you want to . . . ?"

We ended up in the back seat, where Joey did something that made concentrating impossible.

Impossible. I briefly stuttered on trust, battled embarrassment, wondered if his forearms would cramp in that position and thanked heaven that I'd showered with lilac body wash.

"You should text your mom," I choked out. "Let her know where you are."

He stopped what he was doing to smile up at me. "Now?"

Valid point. "Never mind. Network's probably overloaded."

"Wait," Joey said. "Was that a 'No, don't do that anymore' or an 'I'm not sure'?"

"Not a no." I bent one arm behind the back of my head to cushion it. The damn shoulder belt kept catching on my hair. "More like an attack of over-responsibility."

One more wrong word, and I'd kill the mood entirely.

"How about a 'Yes, please, Joey?'" I added. "How's that?"

"Works for me." He dropped a kiss on my hip bone. "Don't you just love tornadoes?"

I'm still not sure what he got out of it. But I had no doubt that Joey had forgiven me, no doubt that he'd accepted all of who I am. And together, we weathered the storm.

No Place Like It

We talked. We listened. In stops and starts, then as steady as the pouring rain.

He talked more than I did because I'd already had so much of my say.

"It's like you were so busy trying to patch things up that you never stopped to really think through how what you said had affected me," my boyfriend explained.

He was right. I admitted that, let it sink in deep and kept listening.

Still in the back seat, Joey added, "On the porch, I was shocked. You caught me completely off guard."

He brushed aside a strand of my hair. "Lou, I know you. I've met your family and your friends. I've been in your house. I've seen your mother's ginormous non-fiction collection. I'd already figured out that you're . . . Muscogee? Or, uh, Native at least."

He'd been paying attention, echoing the words I'd used to define myself.

"I'd obviously fallen for you," Joey said. "Being Native is a big part of who you are. So why would you think I'd have a problem with that?"

I liked hearing that he'd fallen for me. Shifting my head on his bare shoulder, I agreed with Joey that, yes, we had been fine. Better than fine. But not everyone thought the way he did. I'd needed reassurance, especially after having dated Cam.

Joey said he honestly hadn't thought much about Indigenous people, but he had zero problem with us and was open to learning more and, by the way, he could happily live the rest of his life without ever hearing Cam Ryan's name again.

We found our way back to laughter, then desire, then, finally, to peace.

Our jeans hadn't had time to dry, and, in the tight space, they were a bitch to yank back on. "Want to invite your mom to my cousins' house for dinner?" I asked.

"You sure?" Joey replied. "Your family wouldn't mind?"

I sucked in my belly to zip. "Uh, really, no. Everybody's welcome. Shelby will be there with her dad. And the Headbird family, too."

Joey managed to pull himself together enough to text his mom and three-point turn the car around. We hadn't parked in a space per se—they'd all been full. Instead, he'd taken the opening in front of an exit door, leading to the stairs.

The radio station was playing "Jingle Bell Rock."

"I was just thinking." Joey steered his Jeep up the incline. "Last Christmas, I stayed at my dad's crash pad in Kansas City and we did presents in the morning. Then he dropped me off at our old house in Overland Park and I went through the motions all over again with Mom."

The next song up was "O Tannenbaum." I thought of the blessed relief I'd felt earlier when I'd confirmed that my family was still safe and whole.

A different kind of storm had changed Joey's life forever. Having faith in the two of us was probably hard for him, too, for his own reasons. It was important for me to remember that.

He added, "My sister had ditched all of us to go skiing with a bunch of her college friends in Winter Park, Colorado." We rounded a concrete pillar. "It wasn't the worst day of my life, but it didn't feel like . . ."

"A holiday?" I'd sort of assumed his parents were an interfaith couple, his mom Christian and his dad Muslim. Somewhere along the way, I'd picked up that unmarried Muslims probably weren't supposed to do what we'd just done in the back seat, but it's not like unmarried Christians were supposed to, either. Or, on second thought, I'd never heard a peep in church on that specific subject, so maybe it was open to interpretation.

I dearly hoped it was open to interpretation.

As the Jeep exited the garage, I risked the question. "Do both of your parents believe in, uh, Christmas?"

"For sure," Joey said. "Personally, I'm more of a spiritual guy than a religious guy, but me and Santa are tight. Why?"

Turkey Trotters had begun to cautiously emerge from their shelters, their eyes to the clearing sky. The rain and hail had stopped. The sun was peeking out from behind the clouds. But the run was obviously cancelled.

"No reason," I replied, using my phone to quickly and covertly do a search for Lebanese Christians, which, apparently, there are plenty of. In fact, most Arab Americans are Christians.

I had no desire to fumble another conversation, so I left it at that.

It struck me, not for the first time, how much I didn't know that I didn't know.

Ping! Emily had sent me a smiley face and a turkey emoji.

I responded with a thumbs-up emoji, *L+J,* and a red heart emoji.

A moment later, she sent a close-up selfie of herself and Rebecca, cheek to cheek, with beaming smiles and a red heart emoji of their own.

From the looks of things, the storm had grown worse before subsiding. Plummeting hail had dented vehicles, cracked and broken windshields. It littered the parking lot. The race banners, water dispensers, little paper cups, and reception tent were strewn all over the place.

As for the outdoor mall, the landscaping had taken a hit. But aside from a few broken windows, the buildings were intact, the walls standing, the roofs where roofs belonged.

Ping! Joey's mom texted that she'd love to come to dinner. I grabbed his phone, sent my cousins' street address, and said we'd meet her there after checking on my house.

Then, using my own phone, I texted my cousin Rain, telling her to expect more company.

Ping! Ping! Karishma texted Joey and me both, asking if we were safe and if we'd cover the storm for the *Hive*. Our answer of course was yes.

"I can salvage footage from the Trot," Joey said. "I also shot the pre-race crowd before I saw you. We can use it to open our story on the tornado."

Joey and I drove to my subdivision. On the way, he pulled over to the side of the road and, without a word, we traded places. He lowered the passenger-side window and turned on his camera. I took the wheel.

Moving on, he shot fallen tree trunks and hefty branches, some partly blocking the street. Water pooled in low-lying areas. A doghouse had been blown to pieces.

Joey kept bitching about the equipment he didn't have with him. I could tell he was still quietly kicking himself for not filming the twister itself. That he longed to stop along the way, take his time, but I had to hurry. I needed to report in to my family.

So far, it could've been worse. The residential damage seemed more on par with a severe thunderstorm. But twisters are capricious. They'll level a home and spare the one next door.

Beyond the Emerald Hills entrance, the sugar maples along the avenue had taken a beating. A play structure had careened to one side. The *New Homes for Sale* signs were missing.

I swerved to avoid a portable grill in an intersection.

On my cul-de-sac, we spotted two brown terriers from down the street, gingerly making their way out from under another neighbor's deck, and returned them to their relieved owners.

Moving on, at the house across from mine, the bubbler fountain had toppled, cracked.

I could already hear chain saws—just in time for firewood season.

I'd briefly forgotten about the paint on my garage door until Joey pulled into my driveway. The plastic sheet Daddy had hung over it had blown into our front lawn.

"There is no place like home."
Go back to where you came from.

"Is there something you want to tell me?" Joey asked, eyes wide.

"Walk and talk." Getting out of the Jeep, I launched into a recap, leaving Daniel, Peter, and the failed arson attempt out of it. "You can check out Alexis's article and my editorial in Tuesday's special issue of the *Hive*." We circled the property, surveying for damage.

"The one time I skip reading my own school newspaper." He glanced down at me. "I mean, *our* school newspaper."

"Ours," I agreed. "At first, the families decided as a group to keep quiet about what was going on." A curved, thick branch teetered on the corner of my garage roof.

"Are you mad that I didn't say anything before?" I asked, storing the newly folded plastic sheet beneath a chair on the porch. "You know, since we were covering the story for the *Hive*?"

Joey dropped a reassuring kiss on the top of my head. "I'm mad at whoever went after Hughie and his friends like that. I wish you'd felt like you could've come to me."

I wanted to say it was all behind us now. I did have hope that Daniel's conversation with Pastor Ney would make a difference, but . . . "People like that, they're not going anywhere."

Joey squared his broad shoulders. "Neither are we."

I texted Mama reassuring photos. Our new home was safe, secure, down to the very last hobbit hole, though the tiny ceramic turkeys had been lost to the wind.

Giving Thanks

Joey and I followed the rainbow to my cousins' yard, transformed for the festivities—picnic tables, heat lamps, bulb lights strung from tree to tree. Mason jars of sunflowers.

Half the neighborhood was already there. Everyone with their own story to share, I was sure, though power had been restored and old town had been spared the brunt of the storm.

The gravel driveway was full. A half dozen cars and trucks crowded the side yard.

Joey left the Jeep parked all the way down the dead-end street.

As we approached, I spotted Dmitri and Marie carrying out platters of food, Hughie tossing horseshoes with Shelby. The puppies frolicked in the grass with Rain's black Lab.

Mama and Daddy waved like they hadn't seen me in years. I waved back.

I love who I am. I love my family, my friends, my Native Nation. I love Kansas. And chances are pretty kick-ass that I love Joey, too.

Pu fvckvkes. We are happy.

My arm circled his waist. His arm circled my shoulders. He asked, "Do Native people believe in Thanksgiving?"

I kissed him. "We believe in gratitude."

Cokvheckv Omvlkat Enakes

As a Kansas teen, I displayed a collection of Oz holiday ornaments in a row on top of my robin's-egg-blue dresser in my bedroom. I loved how much Dorothy loved her home, and to this day, I still think flying monkeys are the stuff of nightmares.

Like Louise, I'm a citizen of the Muscogee (Creek) Nation. I didn't learn about Baum's pro-genocide editorials until I was an adult, and that knowledge came as a blow.

The atrocities committed at Wounded Knee, during removal (also known as the Trail of Tears), and at U.S. federal Indian boarding schools are by no means fully communicated herein. They're referenced in passing as Louise is processing them in the moment. The same is true of tribal sovereignty and U.S. federal American Indian law related to Native children and families.

I strongly encourage readers to seek out official tribal websites and nonfiction by Native and First Nations authors for more information.

Likewise, it's beyond the scope of this novel to fully reflect on the referenced real-world terrorist attacks — the Oklahoma City bombing and the attacks that took place on September 11, 2001 — or their ongoing aftermath. I recommend beginning study at the Oklahoma National Memorial and Museum, the Flight 93 National Memorial, the National 9/11 Pentagon Memorial, and the National September 11 Memorial and/or their respective websites.

In contrast, the televised news stories are fictional. Those familiar with northeast Kansas probably also noticed a few fictional businesses, Joey's fictional previous school (West Overland High), and two fictional towns — (old) Hannesburg and East Hannesburg.

Finally, Louise and Joey's romance is very loosely inspired by my adolescent relationship with the boyfriend to whom this novel is dedicated. I'm grateful for his blessing and support. Although *Louise* is my given middle name, the characters are by no means us. Their story is not our story. However, we do — respectively — share with them a few life experiences and identity elements, including high-school journalism, faith, and heritage.

A quote from L. Frank Baum's novel *The Wonderful Wizard of OZ,* "There is no place like home," is used rather than the more iconic screenplay version because the novel is in the public domain.

Beyond that, attentive readers may have noticed direct or indirect references to Ansel Adams, J. M. Barrie,

Joseph Carlton Beal, James Ross Boothe, Holly Black, E. R. Braithwaite, Libba Bray, Amanda Brown, William F. Brown, Warren Casey, Cecil Castellucci, James Clavell, Rita Coolidge, Carolyn Crimi, Noma Dumezweni, Patrick Sheane Duncan, Robert Eisele, Hal Foster, Gal Gadot, Eric Gansworth, Judy Garland, Woody Guthrie, Jack Haley, Martin Handford, Moss Hart, Jim Henson, Audrey Hepburn, John B. Herrington, Jamie Houston, Rock Hudson, William Hurlbut, Jim Jacobs, Patty Jenkins, the King James Bible, Burt Lancaster, Noel Langley, Queen Latifah, Y. S. Lee, Kermit Love, George Lucas, Rooney Mara, William Moulton Marston, Karen McCullah, Meat Loaf, Billy Mills, A. A. Milne, Lin-Manuel Miranda, H. G. Peter, Jeffrey Porro, Elvis Presley, Rihanna, J. K. Rowling, Florence Ryerson, Tony Scherman, Tom Schulman, William Shakespeare, Mary Shelley, Kirsten Smith, Tim Tingle, J. R. R. Tolkien, Walela, Isaac Watts, Joss Whedon, Laura Ingalls Wilder, Oprah Winfrey, Clare Herbert Woolston, and Edgar Allan Woolf.

Mvskoke

Mvskoke is a living language. Louise, Hughie, and I are beginning rather than fluent speakers. We know common phrases and some vocabulary words.

My sources were the Muscogee Nation (MN) website, the College of Muscogee Nation (CMN) website, and the Mvskoke Nation Language App (MNLA), all of which reflect their own dialect, spelling, and pronunciation decisions. They also offer audio files featuring the proper pronunciation of the incorporated words and sentences.

The Wolfe siblings reference using the app, but it's not their only learning source.

Mvskoke-English Glossary

Vca fvckes: I am happy (MNLA/Describing People)

Cokv kerretv heret os: Learning is good (CMN)

Cokvheckv omvlkat enakes: Education for all (CMN)

cvtv hakv: blue bread (MNLA/Traditional Food)

Estonko?: How are you? (MN)

Estvmin like cet towa?: Where do you live? (MN)

Here mahe: I'm doing fine (MN)

hesci: hello (CMN)

hotvle rakko: tornado (MNLA/Nature)

Lekothe tos: It is warm (MNLA/Weather)

mvto: thank you (MNLA/Words)

Oren hiye tos: It is very hot (MNLA/Weather)

Pu fvckvkes: We are happy (MNLA/Describing People)

Yvhiketv cvyace tos: I like to sing (MNLA/Action Phrases)

Mvto

Hearts Unbroken took me longer to complete than any of my previous novels.

I recall mentioning the project to fellow author Uma Krishnaswami eight years ago, adding, "But of course I could never write that."

I wasn't ready, and the world wasn't ready, either.

She replied that I wouldn't always be the same writer I was that day. I'd grow.

Young adult publishing isn't static. It would change, too.

Today I'm heartened, optimistically unbroken, and a believer in the power of Story.

My thanks to Hilary Van Dusen, my insightful editor; Ginger Knowlton, my literary agent of twenty years; Deborah Noyes, who originally acquired this manuscript; Hannah Mahoney, the copyeditor; and Pamela Consolazio, the jacket designer. I also greatly appreciate the support of the talented teams at Candlewick Press and Curtis Brown Ltd.

In addition, I'm deeply thankful for the efforts of my intern Gayleen Rabakukk, booking agent Carmen Oliver, web designer Erik Neills of Square Bear Studio, and manuscript readers Anne Bustard, Amy Rose Capetta, Cory Putman Oakes, Sean Petrie, Kevin Wohler, and Jennifer Ziegler. (Kevin was the editorial cartoonist on our own Kansas high-school newspaper.)

Thanks also to the AAWs, Austin SCBWI, and the Writers' League of Texas.

More globally, as a faculty member in the Writing for Children and Young Adults MFA program at Vermont College of Fine Arts, I'm blessed to receive continuing education and inspiration. Thanks to my VCFA family for all that you've taught me about writing and myself.

With regard to research assistance and personal insights, I gratefully salute: the Alexander Mitchell Public Library staff in Aberdeen, South Dakota; Teresa Arevalo; Christopher T. Assaf; Varsha Bajaj; Hamilton Beasley; Breed & Co./Ace Hardware of Austin, Texas; Gene Brenek; Joseph Bruchac; Samantha Clark; Ron Clements; the Cohen family; Jenny Kay DuPuis; Ted Elliott; Carolyn Flores; Hannah Gómez; Mette Ivie Harrison; Andrea Henry; Shelley Ann Jackson; Varian Johnson; Johnson County Community College; the Lawrence Free State High School registrar; the City of Lawrence, Kansas, communications department; Kevin Noble Maillard; Jenny Moss; John Musker; S. D. Nelson; Lisa Palin; Aaron Rittmaster; Terry Rossio; Tracy Russell; Lisa Shafer; Greg Leitich Smith; Traci Sorell; the United States Department of Justice Civil Rights Division (ADA); Carol Lynch Williams; and Owen Ziegler.

On a more personal level, many of the above, plus

William Alexander, Salima Alikhan, Kathi Appelt, Joy Castro, Elizabeth Cole, Robin Galbraith, David Macinnis Gill, Michael Helferich, Lindsey Lane, Cynthia Levinson, April Lurie, Kekla Magoon, Liz Garton Scanlon, Don Tate, Jo Whittemore, Kathryn Zbryk, and, finally, KU journalism educator and one-time *Kansas City Star* editor Tom Eblen, who died during the writing of this novel.

Rest in peace, Tom. You were a stellar teacher. If this novel inspires one teen to someday study journalism, all the credit goes to you.